Why The Hell Didn't You Tell Me?

Cover drawing inspired by Johannes Hevelius 1611-1687

Why the Hell Didn't You Tell Me?

By Steven Bach

Illustrated by
Steven Bach

Published by: HAPPY CREEK ARTISANS
SEYMOUR, TENNESSEE

Library of Congress Control Number: 2009937763
ISBN-13: 978-0-9842582-0-8
ISBN-10: 0-9842582-0-5

PRINTED IN THE UNITED STATES OF AMERICA

Acknowledgments

My heartfelt thanks to my family, friends, and the many people I don't know who helped me get into, through, and out of this exciting portion of my life. Thanks to Sarah Mate and Carol Terrell for their proofreading. And I especially thank my wife who has loved me in the aftermath.

Contents

Introduction

As a youngster I was taught that the world around me was finished, and that it just needed exploring. Life experiences have revealed a much more mobile, chaotic, and complex world. My concept of infinity has become infinitely larger several times. I will try to refrain from inserting comments about what I have now come to believe; but just let the tale of ignorance, idiocy, and egomania unfold.

I am calling this a work of fiction for lack of any other standing. Many of these experiences happened under the influence of drugs, alcohol, stress, or a mixture of all three, so some are hallucinatory. They are true in the sense that when they happened to me, I thought that they were real. In retrospect, I may be of two minds. As for the sober, seemingly factual parts, they are entirely fictional. The characters encountered in "real" life are entirely fictitious. So, anything in this account that resembles reality is purely coincidental, while the episodes which appear absolutely impossible and totally hallucinatory are entirely true.

Finally, I have to say keeping a journal as these experiences unfolded would have been the ideal way to report them, though impossible, given the varied altered states of mind, the long periods of chaos and general wandering in the wilderness, the brushes with the law, homelessness, excursions with bears, dogs, police, sentient weather systems, ancient star constellations, unknowable entities, and what not. Stopping to make journal entries was out of the question. There were no time-outs. So this is a retroactive journal of excursions outside the construction of illusions generally accepted as reality that took place in a two year period over thirty years ago.

Why The Hell Didn't You Tell Me?

To Esther

Secret to Everything

Those who know do not tell
Those who tell do not know.

                              Lao Tse

I once discovered the answer to everything. The elusive unified 'It' came as an instantaneous flash. The idea my mind was mulling over consisted of two tape recorders stacked one atop the other. The top one was recording a copy of the tape running through it onto another tape, which was coming out of it. The bottom recorder was adding the data from an in-going tape onto its through-tape. I don't believe it was also erasing the through-tape before recording on it. There was no doubt that the tapes and Input/Output units were reproducing like rabbits, and in no time the entire sky was pulsing with

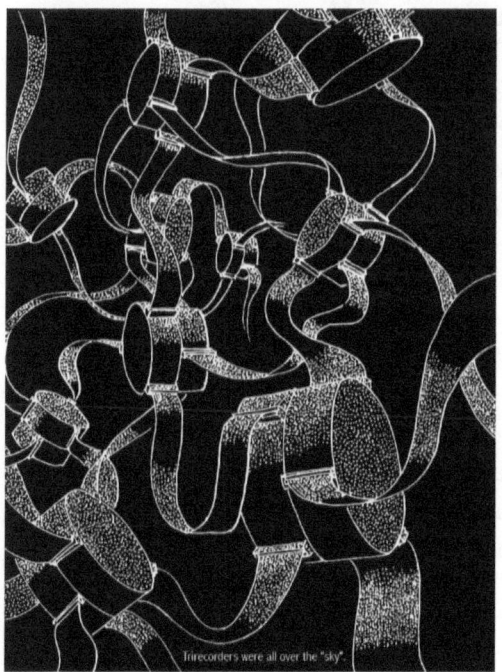

data. Suddenly the secret to everything became clear to me! My whole being changed from seeking to knowing in an instantaneous flash of insight. I was outside my house and marveled at how everything fit together so elegantly. It was all so simple! The sky, the tree branches, and the electric wires, still shiny and wet from the recent rain, looked so beautiful. The images seen by my mind's eye covered the whole sky with recorders and tape.

Everything made perfect sense. I ran back inside and shouted to my guests.

"I've found the secret to everything!"

They all looked at me, some of them with expressions of great expectation, and some with expressions of "Oh shit, here he goes again." I raised my hand with my index finger pointing up to both emphasize my thought, and also to focus everyone's attention. I opened my mouth to speak, and immediately began to feel a flow of glowing white light accelerating rapidly through my brain and spinal column. It was as if a three-foot wide tape were running through my body from left to right. In my x-ray-like vision a stack of black blocks represented my skull and the vertebrae of my spinal column. Like heads in a tape recorder, the blocks were reading information from the multi-track white tape and feeding it to my body and brain. But, as the rapidly accelerating tape outpaced the block's ability to read from it, they began to race to keep up. My spinal column flew to the right and carried my consciousness away with it. I collapsed and crumpled in a spineless heap onto my right side. Almost immediately, another set of black blocks came from the left, bearing a new central nervous system, which snapped into place and restored my consciousness to an instant before I fell over.

Sitting back up I said something like, "WOW, that was just incredible!"

I tried to speak again, and just before I could utter a word, I collapsed again. My consciousness was replaced click, click, and clack as the blocks stacked up another me. Getting up and trying yet another time to speak the whole and simple truth, I was knocked down again and replaced.

Finally I said, "Sorry, I can't put it into words. As soon as I try to form the words my consciousness gets carried off and is replaced with me as I was an instant before I tried to speak."

So there I was, living in ignorance of what I once knew completely, The All, the secret of EVERYTHING. I think though, that there were two or three of me who went into wherever that knowledge might be. I guess the rule is: "If you know, you go."

Helicopter Falling

One morning a friend and I walked out of the kitchen onto the back porch with our mugs of coffee to stand and muse over the fresh spring day. As we stood there admiring the beautiful sunny morning with the dandelions blooming in the lawn, and the maple leaves waving gently in the breeze, a helicopter came over the ridge and began noisily hovering, and hovering, flappa, flappa, flappa, shattering the tranquil morning. I looked up at it and thought, "That damn thing ought to fall out of the sky," and then went back into the house for more coffee.

Almost immediately, my friend came running in and said something like, "Holy Shit, that helicopter just landed right out there!"

I looked out the window and sure enough the helicopter was sitting in the neighbor's yard about fifty feet from my kitchen window. I thought, "My God! What just happened? Did I somehow link to a higher self or power?" We reached the helicopter as a very pale man in a suit was climbing out clutching his briefcase. I was still pretty concerned with the ramifications of this wishing, and the almost immediate grounding of the helicopter, so I didn't know what to think much less say when I recognized the man climbing out of the door as one of the town's prominent businessmen. The pilot was pretty concerned about his unscheduled landing, and said he didn't understand what had happened. He had hit a down draft, and even with the power on full, he had barely cleared the neighbor's roof before slamming into their yard while just missing trees on every side. Maybe I really had caused it! After a quick inspection, and finding no damage other than a bent skid, the pilot said he had better get back in the air before the police arrived and forced him to file an accident report.

The pilot asked the businessman, "Do you want to

4

fly back in the helicopter?"

"No," he rasped, almost shouting, "There's no way in hell I'd get back in that thing!"

Turning to me he asked. "Can you give me a ride home?"

"Sure." I said.

"Well, I have GOT to get out of here! I'll call you later," yelled the pilot, as he revved the helicopter's engine.

"Fine, I'll call you later today." The businessman shouted as the helicopter shot up and away.

"There's no way in hell I'd get back in that thing," He muttered under his breath, shaking his head.

"Are you ready for a cup of coffee and a doughnut?" I asked, nodding toward the house.

"Sure. You know, I used to live in this house when we first moved to town."

"No, I didn't. Welcome home again." I said.

We settled down at the kitchen table and talked. It turned out that he had been checking on the view from an observation tower he was planning to build when the helicopter just came down. I didn't want to tell him that I had wished it would fall out of the sky because it was disturbing the peace. Instead, I mentioned that some time ago my wife and I had opened the space under the stairs to make a small meditation room. We hoped to use the room to tap into some universal consciousness from time to time, or to at least take a nap. The space had been full of stuff that had fallen through the cracks.

He then told a story about an inexpensive cameo ring he had brought home to his daughter from his army stint in Europe during World War Two. His daughter had felt terrible about losing the ring the day after he had given it to her. After a thorough search of the house they had decided that it might have fallen through a crack in the stairs. Though it had little monetary value, it had great sentimental value.

Had we by any chance found it under the stairs? Yes, I was happy to say, we had found it. I gave it to him so he could give it back it to his daughter. So, thirty years later, after falling from the sky to retrieve it, he was able to return his daughter's ring.

Was this unscheduled, inexplicable helicopter landing, and recovery of the long lost ring a mere coincidence, or was it that Jungian phenomenon called synchronicity, a unifying force beyond comprehension, bringing things together in unlikely ways? Could it be that we're all enmeshed in several alternate realities simultaneously occupying the same space? The more immediate question to me was what role, if any, my wishing had played in all of this?

Synthetic Psilocybin

Curious about expanding my consciousness to find some answers to the Big Questions, I began to think about sampling some recreational chemical compounds. I didn't have to wait long. The next afternoon some good friends brought over some synthetic psilocybin, a synthetic mushroom compound. They looked like they were having a great time, laughing and giggling as they lay in a heap on a pile of broken concrete blocks. It seemed like a real jolly chemical, so after they left, and with my wife and the kids in their beds fast asleep, I thought I would try some. I was a bit worried. This was to be the first time I'd tried a really active hallucinogen, and even though I'd seen my friends having great fun, I really didn't know what to expect.

I swallowed the little blue and green spotted rascal. It was bitter. About thirty minutes later it began to take effect. It was cold wintertime and although I had a fire burning in the wood stove, I began to feel chilly. I wondered if I should just get in bed, but after deciding that my tossing and turning would keep my wife awake I stayed close to the wood stove and listened as the fire crackled and the other sounds of the house grew more and more interesting. The sounds seemed to be synchronized with my thoughts. For instance, I would be thinking of a bird flying and begin to see it in my mind's eye approaching the real plane, (what the physical eye could see). As it came into the real plane, its energy would concentrate in the stove and make the fire crack and sparks fly. Or sometimes the energy wouldn't concentrate so much, and the boards in the house would creak as though buffeted by a gentle but firm wind.

After about an hour had passed, the chilly feeling turned into a tensed-muscle, clenched-teeth, jittery feeling. I watched my hand for about twenty minutes, and thought that this must be what babies are doing when they stare at their hands for so long. I got up and went to the bathroom to piss. What wonderful bubbles! My face in the mirror looked pretty good until I smiled and saw my teeth. They looked yellow stained, and they had vertical cracks in them. Was this how they would look when I got old? I remembered that years ago my father had said that if you stare into a mirror for about an hour you would see some very strange things. I went back downstairs, sat in a stuffed chair, and just stared at the room. A crumpled paper bag under the table first started glowing as if it was about to burst into flames with no smoke, then the image settled down and began to look like a spherical TV or a crystal ball with scenery changing inside it. I wondered if it would look like that if I just stared at it for an hour without doing drugs.

Eventually, I decided to go outside to check out the workshop. I don't remember the workshop very much, it was over 30 years ago, but I remember I lay down in the driveway to look at the stars, and that I had to remind myself to breathe once in awhile in order to stay alive. I didn't feel that I had to beat my heart though, so I guess my autonomic nervous system was still doing most of its work. I didn't feel the cold or much of anything else for that matter. This was not alarming to me at the time, just a dispassionate observation, but I eventually decided that if I didn't get up and go into the house where it was warm I would freeze to death.

Once I was back inside, I began to worry that maybe, since I couldn't really feel anything anymore, I would stoke the wood fire too high, and burn the house down. Or I might make some other terrible mistake. After much consideration, I decided that I would be fine if I left everything alone, and went to bed as usual. After all, it had always worked before, so I headed upstairs for the bedroom.

When I reached the top of the stairs I began to have hallucinations. The old-age teeth and the glowing bag were just minor. This was complete. First there was a landscape not unlike the woods in the hollow behind my house in late spring. The stairs had become a little over-grown gully, or small ravine, with a path leading down to a flat area. There was vegetation all around, and I felt as though I could walk into the area and all would be congruent with my "real" world. Then the picture or screen shifted, sort of like a TV does when the vertical control is not adjusted right, and the picture changed to a desert scene with a steep, rocky path leading down through a small canyon under a night sky full of stars. Again all I had to do was to walk on in. I was afraid to do that though, for fear I wouldn't ever find my way back to my "real" world which was two levels below this one. So, I thought back down two levels, and sure enough, there in front of me was the old familiar stairway in my old familiar house. I thought back up to the desert, but went too fast, and over-shot it by about three levels to a city scene with a brick stairway. Then down, then up and oh my God, there were thousands of these levels, some on other planets, some even built of the stars themselves. Zipping up and down, playing, I would see my familiar stairway pass by every so often. Once the prospect of getting lost in another reality was not as much of an issue as I thought, I explored up and down for awhile, still not walking more than a few steps into the other realities for fear of becoming lost in them, then I found my own familiar stairway, walked into my familiar reality to the bed, and dreamed I don't know what.

I suspected that this type of experience was what the Chinese sages were referring to when they talked of the world being like an onion, or a lotus blossom with different layers. Or the meaning of those Chinese balls carved of ivory with the many different layers. Maybe those balls depict what was happening in the different layers at the time of some particular historical event.

Alternate Reality

This would not be the last time I experienced an alternate reality. A few weeks later, we had some friends over for dinner. In the course of the evening I drank a large quantity of scotch and then went to bed. Sometime later, in a dream, I was driving on the Blue Ridge Parkway, slowing down often to take in some really spectacular scenes, such as tall waterfalls, amazing rock formations, and breathtaking vistas of forests and valleys. I was frustrated that I hadn't brought along any of my cameras. At one point, I had to pull over to relieve myself. I got out of the little convertible, walked around the front of it to a bush, and started to piss.

My wife hollered and glared at me from the car, "Steven, what the hell are you doing?"

Looking at her in amazement, I said, "What does it look like? I'm pissing!" Then, I got back into the car with her and drove away.

The next morning my wife wasn't speaking to me, which was very unusual. I kept asking her what was wrong. Finally, she said I knew what was wrong, which of course I didn't. At last, after much pleading, she told me that I had gotten up, walked around the bed to the antique washstand where we kept the diapers, and pissed all over it. And when she had asked me what the hell I was doing, I'd said, exactly like I had replied in my dream, "What does it look like? I'm pissing," then walked back around the bed, got in, and went to sleep.

No wonder she was angry.

Telepathy

I always wanted to be able to be telepathic with others. I remember lying with my girl friend, gritting my teeth, and trying to force my thoughts into her head.

She said, "You're trying too hard; you need to relax."

I didn't know what she meant. Later I found out that I was being telepathic with others quite frequently.

My English teacher said that I and a friend of mine had written in-class papers that were almost word for word. She thought we were trying to pull another one of our pranks, so she had never mentioned it.

I took a proposal to some businessmen in town to make a shopping center with different fronts on all the stores. They looked shocked at the time, and after they built it, I thought they had stolen my idea. But, I now think I had just picked up on their idea, or that I had shared my mind with them.

Back then, I used to drive too fast. Sometimes I would slow down for no reason, go around a curve, and come upon a wreck, or a police car, or road construction. Some of the time I saw somebody blinking their lights as a warning, but many times that didn't explain it. I almost never got a speeding ticket.

My driving slowed down considerably after I began to think that the people in the wrecks I came upon were really me and my friends in a slightly different universe.

One night a friend of mine brought his new wife over. We were all playing with those telepathic testing cards with the x, o, +, and whatever on them. Most of us were just achieving the expected percentage until his wife and I tried it. We got about 20 in a row. I think my friend got a little angry with us for connecting so well.

On the way to the beach my girlfriend and I stopped at Duke University to visit their parapsychology department. While there, we took a test that was on a computer. If I remember correctly, the object of the test was somehow linked to a random number generator. Anyway, I remember imagining two contra rotating, numbered wheels and I was able to hit the numbers pretty good and even got disgusted when I was wrong before the computer told me I was wrong. Much later, while learning computer programming, I came across a random number generator that used programmed loops in much the same way. My girlfriend and I both did pretty well on the tests.

In the afternoon I was invited to sit in on their monthly meeting. I don't remember much of it because most of it had to do with their finances, but I do remember one man said that they needed some new computers and while pointedly looking at me he said, "We all know the limitations of the Apple IIs we are using." After which, most of the people there chuckled. As we were leaving they asked if we could come back for further testing.

One of the books I had read was, I believe, "The Magic of the Senses." It might have been one of the Time Life series books. The book explained that the picture we see with our eyes is not put together until the information from a bunch of individual sensors in our eyes is compiled by our brain into an image. It occurred to me that life is complex enough that with telepathy one could patch together an image by using input from a sensor here, perhaps from a frog, another input there, from a bug, and so on until an image was built making up a distributed body. Maybe this could explain how another universe could appear to exist and seem so real while hallucinating, or explain how ghosts could exist.

Visit with the Ladies

I went over to the house of some young ladies with whom I was quite smitten, and we took some acid just after dark. While the acid was taking effect, we sat on the front porch and watched the bugs as they buzzed around a security light on the electric pole by the driveway. Soon a bat was slurping them up on a regular basis.

Some background might help here. First, you need to know that there had recently been some pictures in one of the popular nature magazines about how bats pirouette around a bug as they catch it. Secondly, you need to know that just a few days back I had needed to attach something high on an electric pole. I had thought that maybe I could climb it like a Hawaiian does when going after a coconut, or like an iron worker going up a column. It had worked on the pole at home which wasn't as high as the one at the ladies' house. So, partly from the curiosity of seeing the bat food-dance close up, and partly from thinking I could impress these young beautiful women, I walked up the pole. The climb up that higher pole nearly exhausted me, so I couldn't stay up there for more than a half-dozen brief passes of the bat before having to come down or fall down. Distracted as I was by hanging on to the pole with my last bit of energy, the glimpses of the bat dining on bugs that I saw were not as impressive as the pictures in the magazine I had seen from the safety of my couch. Damn! Those nature photographers are fast. My memory shows my glimpses as kind of blurry videos, not the nice clear still shots like were in the magazine. And not one word from the ladies about my pole-climbing abilities, just some odd looks sort of like the time when I said, "Watch this," stripped naked, and did a pantomime of taking off my birthday suit. I grabbed a fold of skin at my waist and worked it up my body with both hands, and then down my arms and over my head. Then, I grabbed a fold of skin at my waist and worked it down my legs and off my feet. Anyway, I got the same look. I thought it looked pretty good in the mirror. I put my clothes back on but not my birthday suit.

Later on I was sitting on the roof. I think we had eaten dinner because I remember being able to look through time and the house at the recent dinner-eating glowing down there in the kitchen. Looking at the cars in the drive, I remembered my sister and brother telling me about their trip to the Studebaker plant. They described seeing different parts of cars coming down the assembly line. Phantom parts of cars flowed out of the woods around the house, and assembled themselves into the cars in the driveway. It was easy to envision the past, but the future was not so easy.

One of the girls sat down beside me and told me that the other was sick and had gone to bed. I looked through the house and saw her in bed sick. When I looked back, the view from the roof looked like the set from an old opera. The clouds, the trees, the cars, the whole picture seen through my eyes, looked like cutouts of artfully painted cardboard waving in the psychic breeze. I looked at the girl and said, "It's all cardboard!" She said something that translated as Harrumph and left.

As I sat there meditating, I remembered a story in a sci-fi magazine in which the navigators of space ships would fly between stars and galaxies in far outer space by stretching their gossamer wings across the almost infinite distances and then pulling the space ships from one place to another. Instead of flying a space ship, I spread my imaginary wings, reached for the sky, and then pulled my astral body along and up into the stars. Then the world and I seemed to be made entirely of stars. Once in this starry world I relaxed. I was feeling the beauty of everything I saw, and briefly wondered how the girls were. Feeling the power in my body, in my wings, and in my mind, I thought they would probably be thinking I was power tripping.

OK You Son of a Bitch, Draw

Then out of the ether from around me but mostly from the left, and below, an entity came into my body and loudly growled, "OK you son of a bitch, draw." Then, with his mind, he installed a bundle of wires and cables into my body. He spliced some to my brain; some to my neck and to the nerves in my spinal cord, and some were installed near my shoulder blades close to where the imaginary wings had been attached. He then indicated that he had installed an extra "arm" to reach behind "the veil" so I could manipulate the universe. Though he didn't say it, he also indicated that since I was so intent on messing with the universe that I should just go ahead and mess it up. He quickly taught me to reach behind and touch the sky from the back side and make a visible dot with the finger of my phantom hand. Then he was quiet. Very impressed, I gingerly reached up and touched the back of the sky. It moved. A fuzzy spot pushed toward me.

Somehow, this triggered thoughts as if they were in the form of headlines, like:

Greed and Power;

Corporate and Government Shells for Sale;

A picture of "Me, the Most Powerful Person on the Earth;"

Free Trip to God.

I reached up, touched the sky again with my "behind the veil" arm, and saw the dot my finger made appear between two stars. I thought, "Watch it! This might be able to wipe out a whole star at once!" I dodged the stars as I brought my finger down close to the horizon, nearing a tree. The entity that was still watching in my body said, "Go ahead. Push the tree over." This much power and responsibility overwhelmed me and I screamed, "NO!" and reaching behind my neck, I pulled out the wires, stopping just in time to leave a few thin ones attached, because I also really wanted to say yes.

Dream

At the edge of a parking lot in a mature forest, the shrink's office stood on stilts, a ramp for the handicapped curving up to its shingled egg shape. I climbed the ramp, entered the reception room, and waited for my appointment. After a few minutes of sitting with nothing to read, I realized that I was the only one there. Past the reception counter I found the consultation room. It was decorated like a hamster's cage, but it had furniture and a tread mill instead of a wheel. A bright yellow Plexiglas door led outside to a small lime green plastic deck and from the deck a clear red plastic tube slid me to a gentle landing in a park-like forest.

The forest floor was mowed or swept, and after an easy walk up a rise and through the trees, I reached a sunny meadow. I hiked up the grassy hill to a railroad for commuter trains which was under construction. The tracks went straight west over the horizon toward Knoxville, and were part of the preparations for the World's Fair. As I walked back down the field toward some buildings, I noticed that cars were parked in rows on the grass, and that the meadow was being used as a temporary parking lot. These cars were of models and even of shapes I had never seen before. They looked like the odd cars you might see in a car museum; among them were a red, three-wheeled roadster and a greenish, teardrop-shaped sedan. All of them looked very strange. At the bottom of the field there was a paved walkway leading toward a pavilion.

I stopped at a little pond that had a waterfall, and was planted with water lilies. On the rock wall surrounding the pond there was a basket of cookies. I took one, and started to eat. It was pretty chewy, so I looked at it, and was amazed to see that it was a steel gear. That I had just taken a bite out of a steel gear startled me so much that I began to leave my body. As I left, I gave my body a mental MRI or some such, sort of like the scans that have been shown on some TV programs. My teeth were like the ones in the Bond film, made of some extremely hard metal. My eyes were like the ones in the bionic man film. I was mostly a robot. After I left my body and was flying through space back to my real body, a British voice spoke into my mind saying, "Once again sir, don't worry." I woke up in bed, totally amazed.

House Building

I felt that I was having an increase in personal power but I sure wasn't having an increase in money, so one day when a friend near Chicago called and asked me if I would like to help him build a house, I said yes. I got there on the same day. In the Chicago scene, there were more drugs or at least just as many and we were having a good time being pretty stoned while we were building the house. I remember one day we were eating lunch and one of the crew said, "Look at that!" And there, clearly visible with the third eye, was a white arrowhead. I shot a mental arrow at it, breaking it in two. He looked at me reproachfully and said, "Why do you always have to break everything?"

Always, when you are building a house, the weather is a big deal. Until the house gets under roof the building crew is at the mercy of the weather. My father had been a builder before he started making candles, and he was frequently trying to get us kids to use our imagination to drill holes in the clouds, or to just push that cloud bank over a little so it wouldn't rain on us. One day when we were pulling our boat back from the lake dad got us all to concentrate on holding off the rain till we got home. Sure enough it did hold off until we had the boat under the tarp and then it rained cats and dogs.

Of course, at the house site we tried to hold off the rain until the house was under its roof. One day after having a few days of nice weather, rain was in the forecast. We saw the cloud bank coming towards us, but it parted, surrounded us, and became a tall wall of clouds that formed a circular hole about five miles in diameter and tall enough to reach the blue sky. The sun was still shining. This hole lasted for at least a couple of days. I'm not quite sure this "weather hole" wasn't formed simply because there was so much spiritual energy in the area that clouds couldn't exist. Maybe the lyrics "I've seen sunny days that I thought would never end" were referring to this kind of thing.

Come to think of it, I'm pretty sure I didn't experience rain for about two months after this event, long after the house was up and I was far from Chicago. That's not to say it didn't rain on Chicago, it just didn't rain on me. When it finally did rain on me, I wasn't in Chicago anymore. I danced around in the deluge crying with joy and hollering, "Thank you, God. Rain at last!" This gave some onlookers cause for wonder and amusement while I became soaking wet.

When the stud walls of a house have been stood up and temporarily nailed together it is necessary to plumb them so the house will be all straight and true, and all the rectangular drywall and siding will fit properly. My job one afternoon was to watch the bubble in the level while someone on top of the wall unfastened the walls at each corner and then adjusted the corners until my level indicated they were plumb. Then, at my signal they quickly refasten them in the new position. We did this for a couple of walls, and then something told me that it wasn't necessary for the man on top to do anything. I just had to look at the bubble and move it with my mind till it was in the middle. For the rest of the corners in the house I did it that way and declared it plumb. Then we went home for the day.

The next morning my friend wanted us to plumb the walls again.

I said "Why? We did it yesterday."

"Well, let's just check them again today. OK?"

Of course we all were wondering if anything at all had happened when we plumbed them the previous afternoon. I have to admit I was wondering too. Amazingly, they all checked out plumb.

Cocaine

After a couple of weeks or so, I needed to go back home to take care of some business, probably to make a payment on a note at the bank, so I borrowed a cute little sports car from one of the guys and took off for Tennessee. While I was down there I was talking to some people about how good the drugs were in Chicago. Of course I was sharing what I'd brought with me. Everybody enjoyed the candy, especially the high quality coke, and a few guys said they wanted me to get about ten thousand dollar's worth for them. This was a lot of money for me so I told them I would look into it.

Back to work on the house construction in Chicago, I started to check into the possibility of getting the cocaine and asked just how you make any money doing that. It turns out you just get some good stuff and then cut it by adding an equal part of milk sugar which someone said can be bought at the drug store. So if I got ten thousand dollars' worth I would end up with twenty thousand dollars' worth. That sounded pretty simple. So we went around Chicago sampling different cokes at the homes of various dealers and having fun. We had a local guide, which was helpful, to say the least.

One night while out on the coke search totally stoned as usual, we went to a bar which was packed with people having fun. We had a little trouble getting a refill of drinks because it was so busy, so I went to the bar, found an empty spot and ordered up a refill. A pretty stressed waitress came up and told me that this spot was for wait staff only and I had to go back to my seat. She pointed to a small sign that stated that fact and though she didn't really say so she seemed pretty sure that I was a drunken idiot. I said, "Maybe you ought to make the sign big enough for drunken idiots to see," and took the pitcher back to the table. We continued our drunken idiocy for awhile until one of the guys at the table said, "Hey, look at that sign," and there above the bar was a six foot long spotlighted sign with a glowing arrow saying WAIT STAFF ONLY pointing to the wait staff spot. Even a drunken idiot couldn't miss it now.

Then there was Beauty, loved by everyone including me. She enjoyed the mind trips and all the love. She rode a cute red Honda motorcycle and was keeping someone's huge fish tank happy while he was away.

The next weekend a bunch of us went to the dunes in Michigan. Beauty went too. We went riding around in various four-by-fours and dune buggies snorting coke and drinking beer. We cooked sandy food over an open fire and camped out and Beauty did it with everybody because everybody loved her. One night I was lying by the fire in the middle of the camp, quite jiggly and surrounded with the little orange dots and dashes of strong opiates, when along came Beauty to snuggle. Snuggling was quite nice and she said, "I've made it with everyone else so I might as well with you too," then she got up and left. A little while later she came back dragging a blanket behind her and arching her eyebrows along with everything else. I just lay there in my orange aura and said, "Where are you going?" She just mumbled something matter of factly, not angrily, about my being too-messed-up-to-mess with her and walked on by, even though I really wasn't. It just didn't occur to me that we had any need for privacy other than a blanket. I just kept on looking at the beautiful stars, seeing different constellations, among them the great turtle that my young son had pointed out to me one night while we lay on a different beach. I missed my kids.

Trip to New York

My sons were living just south of NYC and some friends of mine were doing a play in the big city so I decided to go. I guess my car wasn't working or something because I hitchhiked to New York. I took off about midnight and rode the commuter train as far as it would go, to somewhere around Gary, Indiana, and then I got on the interstate to hitchhike. Barely a few minutes passed when a car zooming along passed me, slammed on its brakes, shifted into reverse, and backed up about a hundred yards to me. Fortunately at one in the morning there was almost no traffic. The driver got out of the car, ran over to me and immediately started apologizing for being late. I assured him that it was all right and that really I too had just gotten there. I thought he'd surely mistaken me for someone else, but then again I wasn't thinking too quickly. After getting in the car with the three people they again apologized for being so late and I again told them I didn't know what they were talking about. Then they began to tell me that they were supposed to kill me. For some reason this didn't alarm me. Maybe they did this to everybody they picked up, just for fun, I thought, so I told them, "But, you aren't going to." Then I lay back and took a nap

Sometime later I woke up. We were still driving on the interstate and again they said that they were supposed to kill me. Once again I told them that may be so but that they couldn't because I hadn't done anything bad to them and so they just wouldn't do it. They finally let me out at an intersection somewhere in the flat land of Ohio and the guy I was talking to the most handed me a dime and said, "Well, here's your dime anyway," and off they went. Much later while I was telling this story to my mother she told me that the mob always used to leave a dime on the body so someone could use a pay phone to report the killing.

I guess my next ride thought I wasn't coming because those guys were supposed to have killed me. Anyway, it took forever for the next car to stop. I got so frustrated I finally screamed, "Why am I waiting here so long!" As soon as silence filled the noise of my scream a huge meteor hurtled across the sky towards New York. It must have been tumbling because there were sort of lumps of glowing trail behind it instead of just a streak.

Just before dawn I got a ride with someone in a real hot rod; the engine had a blower that stuck out of the hood and the whole car throbbed with power. I thought, "Oh we'll make up some time now." The man eased up to 55 MPH and drove fifty-five for the rest of the trip into New York. It was absolutely maddening. This man with so much POWER right under his foot kept it so under control. I finally decided that this was yet another lesson from God teaching me to respect power and not to use it just for fun. Some time later I came to realize that God seems to really enjoy some good fun. At last, this fire-breathing dragon of a car tiptoed into Manhattan. I'd made it to the city. I walked over to where the play was to take place and the theater was closed. Since I didn't know where all my friends were staying I went off sightseeing.

I loved riding the Staten Island Ferry and after a subway ride I was standing in line with the evening commuters waiting to get on. About thirty feet in front of me I noticed a young woman with dark hair dressed in a navy blue coat. She turned and our eyes met and we smiled at one another. This smiling exchange happened a few more times before the ferry arrived. As the ferry prepared to leave, we found excuses to get close enough to each other to speak. It was obvious that we were drawn to each other. As we stood outside on the deck enjoying the ride, a thunderstorm of awesome power descended on the ferry; the wind rocked the boat with its gusts, and the rain lashed the walls as we retreated into the cabin until it eased enough for us to go back outside. We were hugging each other, giddy in the ebbing storm as we neared the Staten Island dock. She said that she would dearly love to invite me to her apartment but that you just can't survive if you do that in NYC, and so she simply couldn't. I told her I understood, and we kissed goodbye and looked at each other as the water widened between us.

On the way back the storm had passed, and the water, instead of being whipped to froth, was as smooth as glass. The ferry glided almost silently over the water while Manhattan was reflected in its mirror like surface. The World Trade Center towers and the other tall buildings of the city penetrated the layer of clouds and reached for the moon and stars far above. The whole scene was suffused with a gentle glowing from the millions of city lights and the mist. The crew who had just witnessed the storm, and everyone else who was outside on the decks, stared in silent awe at this beauty.

After leaving the ferry I bought a knish from a vendor and walked sort of aimlessly for awhile until I came to a little park with benches. On the benches were flattened cake boxes with poetry written on them. I sat and read for awhile and they reminded me of the poetry my mother used to write. They were kind of angry if I remember correctly. After I had read quite a few of them, a man came and sat on one of the benches and eventually said that he knew the man who wrote the poetry. I asked him if there was any way I could meet the author, and he said that the poet liked beer, and maybe if I went to get some, he could find him. Well, I went to get some beer and sure enough there was someone else there when I got back. We talked about his and my mother's poetry and drank beer for a couple of hours. He was pretty bitter about the disparity between the haves and the have-nots in the world. I finally went and bought a sub and after sharing it with him, I went to find a place to sleep.

Several of the places that I thought were clean and protected enough to provide some sort of shelter were already taken, but at last I found a nice spot between the rock wall of a church and its hedge and went to sleep. When I woke, it was daylight, and I found I had been sharing the hedge with some birds as they were twittering and jumping around about a foot from my face. About fifteen feet past the birds, a lady woke up on her bench, scowled at me, and snuggled back into her rags. Too early, I guess.

After some people-watching and going through the Guggenheim museum, I went to see if my friends were at the theater. This time they were getting ready for the evening show. In order to help out I agreed to pass out brochures for awhile. A bunch of us distributed the flyers until we ran out of them, and then we began to have some fun by improvising. The play had a lot of improvisation, so it was a natural extension. We did things like write ads on the toilet tissue with a magic marker such that the next 20 or 30 feet would display the ad. The connotation may not have been ideal, but it was still fun. Someone put ads on Ping-Pong balls, filled a top hat with them, and then released them at a busy escalator. We tried to make the statements in a non-permanent manner relating to fun. So we had fun all that afternoon and early evening. Before the play I got real stoned. Every time I smoked I would imagine myself going upward, upward toward a very bright white light. After awhile I would come out of that meditation, open my eyes, and be really high. Though I was pretty stoned and may have been seeing more or less meaning in it than was there, I thought the play went well. After the play there was a cast party. Someone had brought some LSD and I took some of that. I remember wondering why the cast hadn't been glowing like that during the play.

Some of us wandered around the city all night. I remember that lying on the sidewalk at the base of the Trade Center Towers and looking up their sides was a really powerful experience. The sunrise viewed from the

Brooklyn Bridge was most beautiful. I was surprised that the walkway was wooden.

That afternoon I borrowed a car to give some of the cast a ride to the countryside of New Jersey and then, by myself, on to visit my children on the shore. We had about six people in a subcompact car and were a pretty jolly crew. At one point while we were still in the city I violently jerked the steering wheel to the left just in time to avoid a large van coming from the rear. I hadn't seen the van and had no idea why I had evaded it. Two possibilities come to mind. One: someone in the back seat saw it coming and I picked up on that. Two: the person in the van was very psychically powerful and was "sweeping" the road in front of him. In any case I took it as an attack and began evasive maneuvers. I've always loved to drive terribly fast, so with the "attack" as an excuse, off we went zigging, zipping and zagging through the sea of taxis and around the triple-parked cars. On the right side of the otherwise blocked road was a narrow gap between two semis. The sides of the trailers were sort of shimmering like the road does on a hot summer day which I had learned probably meant that I could fit between without hitting them. So we shot through the gap with less than an inch on each side, slowed for the light, ran it safely and felt pretty much out of danger again. I remember one of the people in the car saying, "Man, he sure has his space down."

We rode along into autumn in the countryside of New Jersey. It is amazing how quickly the piled-up buildings shrink in height and thin out letting the garden state live up to its name. The fall was beautiful; leaves whirled in a vortex behind us as we zipped through the sunshine. As we drove along at about fifty miles per hour, a flock of birds played with us on their journey south. The blackbirds swooped down and surrounded the car, flying with us for about a hundred yards before surging forward on their way.

26

My sons were living with their mother not too far away, so after dropping the load of people off at their friend's house, I drove on to see them. Before the visit I took the precaution of thoroughly cleaning the car and any stuff I had with me, so there would be no drugs of any kind to be found. I had a premonition that I was going to be stopped by the police and searched. Well, I remembered to do all that, but I didn't remember to get gas. The fumes ran out next to a little mowed field with a creek in the middle and a mature woods behind it. As I coasted to a stop, a young man on a motorcycle rode out of the woods. He splashed across the creek, drove up the rise to the road and asked me if I was having any trouble. I said I had run out of gas. He told me to get on, and that he would take me to the gas station just up the road.

When we got back, I discovered that I had locked my keys in the car. The young man said no problem, and as he started to work on the passenger door, another car stopped, and the driver asked what the trouble was. Soon a contest was on to see which of them could get into the car the quickest. In less than a minute I was thanking them both for getting me into my car. Even today I take the silly trouble to lock my car.

I stopped at the station and filled the gas tank the rest of the way. Five minutes later I was getting stopped by a state trooper who just wanted to check me out. He wanted to look through my car. And although it wasn't legal, I let him search. I told him that I had just cleaned out all the drugs and alcohol and that he wouldn't find anything. He told me that the only thing that would make police uncomfortable was the steak knife that I used to fix my lunches. Even though it was just a serrated steak knife, it would be better if I kept it in the glove box.

The whole search thing left me feeling that I had official clearance to visit my sons. It turned out that my former wife didn't want my sons to see me, but since she was gone for awhile, their Grandmother let us visit for a short time. When it was time to go, the oldest said he would never forget my visit, and the youngest said he would forget because the time would go quicker that way. I drove away with a heavy heart.

It was time for me to head back to Chicago. I returned the car, thanked everyone, took some more acid that was offered me, and went down to catch the subway to the Washington Bridge and I-80. As I rode the subway north to the bridge the acid really began to kick in and I felt like I was glowing. The other passengers seemed to notice that something was odd about me. At least most of them looked at me pretty funny. I just smiled and let my light shine. By the time I got to the bridge it was about sunset and the clouds were glowing red above the city. I had to walk across the bridge because there was no place on it to catch a ride. Halfway across, I looked back at the city and one huge red cloud looked like a mushroom.

Nyack

After the subway ride and the walk across the bridge I really had to go to the bathroom, so I headed for a restaurant.

Lying in the last rays of the sun was a man about my age who said, "Where have you been? We've been waiting for you."

I said, "I've been walking across the bridge, and have to go to the bathroom."

I went in and used the rest room and when I came out, a car pulled up with two more young men in it. The first man asked where I was heading and I told him Chicago. Before long he talked me into partying with them because he was going to get married tomorrow. We drove north as it got dark. At one time after dark I got hot and rolled the power window down. The other guys complained about the cold and wanted it back up. I said, "No, just leave it down." They tried to roll it up and the window just wouldn't move. The guys got pretty worried about the windows being broken and that they would be not only cold but in trouble. I remember wondering if they had "borrowed" the car from someone. Finally after all their carping I reached over to try my luck at rolling them up. There was a visible spark from my fingertip to the window control, and ta-da, the windows worked again.

It seemed as though I had a lot of power. Everything I said seemed to happen. I'd say, "Hit it," and these three young men were all looking for something to hit. I'd say, "How about that bump in the road." They hit the bump in the road, grateful to have completed the "Hit it" order. They were taking me way too seriously.

We went somewhere to get some beer, and then went on to a bar that the groom wanted to visit. The place was closed and the lights were off. The guys in the front seat got out and disappeared. After waiting for awhile the guy in the back seat and I went in also. We wandered around the nightclub drinking some whiskey until one of the guys said it was getting hot and we should leave. I said I wasn't feeling hot and he said there were more ways than one for something to get hot. I later realized that neither of them was the owner; they had broken into the place.

We left to go to another bar in a nearby city. By now it was getting pretty late so by the time we got to the bar of interest it had closed. The groom and the guy in the front seat got out and discovered the door was locked, gestured to the bartenders inside to open up, got rebuffed, and then kicked the door in. The guy in the back seat with me said, "Holy crap, he just mooned the door." I looked, and the door had arcs of cracked glass coming from the handle area and the glass was held together only by the mesh of wire embedded in the glass. "Mooned? Looks more like a comet to me," I said.

Now that the bar was open we all went in. Inside it took some time for the groom to mollify the bartenders but he finally convinced them that he was getting married tomorrow and wanted everyone in the place to have a double something or another which consists of drinking a small shot of some liquor (I seem to remember it being in large communion cups), and then chasing it with something else. After drinking the shot and chaser I began to feel woozy and the guy next to the groom threw up on the bar. Yuk! For some reason I no longer felt like vomiting. The man on my left took great offense at the vomiting and after some words were thrown back and forth by him and the groom, a man sitting at a table hollered that somebody had a gun. The other patrons who had been sitting at tables started to run out of the place, some of them turning over tables in their haste. It was like a Wild West movie. I was standing right between these two arguing A types and was turning my head back and forth as they spoke. In front of me the bartender was looking very strained and serious. I didn't know who had the gun, but it must have been the guy on my left because he told the guy who threw up to eat his vomit and for the groom to help him. I wondered if this cliche which I heard in high school was really happening or was it just an act, or if I was hallucinating the whole thing. He started to eat and I said, "Good God Almighty, you people are disgusting! I'm not putting up with any more of this crap."

After walking outside and down the street, I began to take stock, and realized that I didn't know what city I was in. I stopped at a newspaper box with a local look, spread out my map on its top, and tried to figure it out.

A dark blue van stopped; two guys got out and one asked, "Where are you going?"

"Chicago," I told him. "How do I get to the interstate from here?" and "Where am I?"

"Nyack." He said. "Interstate's just about a half mile that way," he gestured. "You were just in the bar back there, weren't you?"

"Yeah I was there."

"I want to thank you. You just saved my life back there."

I recognized him as the guy on the left in the bar and disagreed, "I don't think so, I was just standing there."

His friend said, "Come on let's go."

He explained to him, "No, this guy saved my life, and by God he is coming home with us." Then he dragged me into the van.

"As long as he's in there, I'm not getting in," said his friend, crossing his arms.

"We've been tight since grade school man. Come on, get in."

"No." I said. "I'll get out. I just need to find my way to the interstate."

"No, you just stay here," he held my arm.

Then to his balking friend, "You have to trust me this time. I know what I'm doing. This guy's coming

31

home with us."

Eventually we all got into the van, and rode a short way to a street with apartments above stores. We had to climb the stairs in the dark because either everyone was so drunk they couldn't find the light switch or the bulb was burned out. Near the top, hearing talk of what just happened in the bar, I remember someone said something like, "talk about walking through walls," and we were in the apartment. We sat around for a little while, maybe smoking some pot and someone said, "That Beauty must have been really something, look at that fish tank." And there against the wall was a big aquarium like the one Beauty was taking care of. I wondered what exactly he meant by that and how he knew of Beauty but didn't ask him. By now I was tired and ready to sleep, and they insisted that I sleep in the "best bed in the house." After some protestation, I went off to sleep in the "sun room."

The sun light woke me the next morning. It really was a sun room. I gathered my things and without waking the guys lying crashed in the living room, I wrote a thank you note on a matchbook I had gotten from the bar that was probably broken into, left it on the kitchen table, and slipped out. The sign to the interstate was visible from where I emerged from the building and after a quick consultation of my map I found that there really was a Nyack.

The trip back to Chicago must have been uneventful because I don't remember any of it.

Coke Again

When I got back to Chicago, it was time to buy some coke so I called the contacts in Tennessee and got no answer again and again and again. I drove back to Gatlinburg and found that the FBI had been asking everyone questions. No one seemed to want to tell me just what questions. On the way back to Chicago I picked up a hitchhiker who looked just like Jimi Hendrix. He even sang Jimi Hendrix songs mostly under his breath. He stayed at my cousin's house for a few days and we had many a long talk about psychic stuff.

One night while we were talking I could see out of my third eye psychic vines growing all over the place. I thought he could see them too.

He said, "You don't even remember your name do you? Man, you are going to have to go through a nova."

We were standing next to a small airport and I told him that I probably could fly one of those small planes because I used to make so many little rubber band powered ones out of toothpicks and tissue paper. He kept trying to buy some drugs from me. I wondered sometimes if he was a narc. I kept telling him I just didn't have any. It took quite a few days for me to convince him to just go away. After about the second day I felt (didn't say so) some admiration for him for something he said or had done and he said. "That's the first time since we met that you've felt something nice about me."

The day he finally left, he was behind me and I felt sort of wavy faint and thought it was somehow coming from him. I asked him what he was doing and he admitted he was trying a power trip of some sort on me. Then he said I had cancer, of course I said no I didn't. Do too. Do not. Yes. No. We were arguing like little kids.

I told my friends that the people who wanted the coke were spooked because the FBI had been asking questions and that I was afraid that it had been my big mouth that had gotten everyone in trouble and they said, "Oh, shit. They will probably want to kill you."

Later when we were eating steak they asked, "How is the steak?"

I answered, "Just fine,"

They pointed, "Eat that bite,"

I did, and almost immediately became disassociated from my body and started drifting back through the chair. Before I hit the wall which I was afraid I'd go right through, I heard a voice in my head saying, "The race is on," and I hollered for my mother because I was thinking that she knew about stuff like this. The wall did catch me but now instead of being nearly all-powerful I was nearly all embarrassed and weak.

By this time, my friends had all decided that they should get ready for hunting season and until I left all the guys walked around with loaded high-power rifles. I was feeling more and more like my trying to get some drugs to sell in Tennessee had caused everyone nothing but trouble.

I think the next day was the last day I went to work on the house. About lunch time I wandered off for a walk including a jaunt on a golf course where I jumped for joy at being so alive and felt like I was describing DNA twirls in mid air. Later I saw the Beatles doing it in their movie, "Help." I passed some golfers who were looking for their ball and mentally indicated to them that it was over there, where since I had seen it last, a metal fence post and a tuft of grass had grown up next to it. They looked at me funny.

After lunch I took my friend's car on some errand. During some arguing with myself about how much I really needed to go home, I decided it would be all right if I just took my friend's car to go back to Tennessee and so with no further argument I pulled onto the freeway heading south and began picking up speed. After going about a mile I felt like an invisible person had reached around me from the back seat and grabbed my wrists giving them a violent jerk to the right. I took this as a totally unsubtle hint that I should pull to the shoulder of the road. Actually it scared the shit out of me. I didn't feel safe driving another inch because whatever that was it certainly wasn't me. I didn't even feel safe walking. It could have taken control and walked me into moving traffic at any moment. I got out of the car on the passenger side and walked straight away from the car and road, climbed the fence and found a pay phone at a filling station on the other side of the access road. I called my friend's mother, who didn't seem to be too surprised that I wanted to be picked up but was a bit puzzled as to why, considering that there was nothing wrong with the car. She dropped me off at her house and went back to work for the rest of the afternoon. So I was still in Chicago, no closer to Tennessee than before, and apparently inhabited by an entity that could control my body.

Entity

I began to "chat" with the entity who had jerked my arms so forcibly in the car. I started to think of this entity as a he for some reason, and he and I began to have a telepathic conversation. He first tried to convince me that he meant me no harm and that he didn't want me to harm myself either. He wanted me to trust him and said that he could help me. He said that just to show me what he could do, he would "bet" me that I wouldn't see anyone for the next hour. I was in a house situated in a suburb with a fire hall and a high school just across the street. There was an apartment building next door and of course the street out front was pretty busy. So I said sure. He said that the rules were that I couldn't run, walking was OK, that I had to stay in the house, and that I couldn't scream or holler.

I went to the window figuring that I would see some kids playing in the ball field across the road. No kids were out there today. I looked up the road where almost always some firemen were sitting outside just yakking or whatever they did there. No firemen. A car was coming down the road. Darn, there was glare on the windshield. Just when I should be able to see someone's head it was blocked by a bush or pole or something. In car after car the people were blocked from my vision. O. K., someone drove into the apartment building parking lot next door. They parked on the other side of the dumpster, and I couldn't see them get out of the car. My friend's mother came home. Glare on the windshield. I heard her come into the house. I walked toward the kitchen saying, "Hi." She said, "Hi." I got into the kitchen. She slammed the door to the bathroom which connected to the den. I figured she would be coming back into the kitchen so I waited. She went into the den. I walked around through the living room to the den. She went back into the kitchen. I went through the bathroom to the kitchen. She had gone on into the living room. I wasn't running or screaming. I went into the living room and saw the door to her bedroom close. Through the door I asked her if everything is all right. She said yes she was just going to lie down for about an hour. I look out the window. Nothing. I said to the entity, "OK you made your point. I want to see people." He said, "OK." Kids came out of the school building into the playing field, the firemen came back out to sit and smoke or whatever, and a lady came out of the apartment building and got into her car. The sun had set enough that there was no glare on the windshields. How the hell did he do that? He said, "Simple." After that he just let me be for awhile. He was probably giving me time to think about the experience.

By now I was getting pretty pickled with LSD. It was my favorite time of year. The fall colors were in splendor and I went to the lake because I love the water. On the beach I was surprised to see ladybugs crawling all over a large piece of driftwood and completely covering it with their bodies. Maybe they were gathering to hibernate. When I got back to my friend's house late that afternoon, the sun's rays were nearly horizontal, and the golden trees were full of singing birds gathering for their flight south. I walked around watching and listening to them until dusk. Just before dark, they let me come right up to their tree and watch with my face touching the leaves as they chirped and hopped from branch to branch always restless. Sometimes they flew to another tree, not frightened, only restless. After dark the moon lit my way, and a light breeze rustled the leaves to set the birds in the trees atwitter again. I was feeling that God made the whole arrangement all for my enjoyment; it was so very beautiful.

A bolt of mental energy carrying the record of my soul's life through time impaled my psyche and ego. As the vision imploded upon me from all directions, I could see a map of my soul's past lives traced through time like lightening with little branches depicting different lives of various interests. Thousands of years were represented and I felt that this was the first time my eyes were opened wide enough to see this large of a picture. For all those thousands of years all of THIS had been surrounding me and I had never noticed it.

I was completely awed by the immensity of this

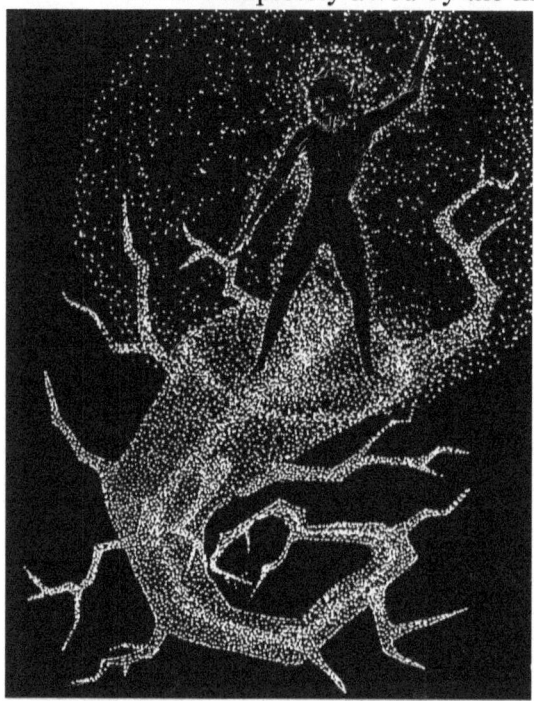 vision and what it seemed to mean, and I wondered if this was my life flashing before my eyes just before my death.

Later that night I went for a walk and the same entity from the "non-visible people" episode began to walk "with" me. I was on a path in a field of tall weeds and came upon a drainage ditch or creek cut straight across the field and the path. I really wanted to cross it without wading in the water and the entity said,

"Go to the left." So I did. The weeds were about waist high in the field and over my head close to the ditch. When I had gone about 300 feet along the ditch he said,

"You can cross here," and indicated the high weeds. I didn't see a path or any evidence that anyone or anything had gone that way so I asked,

"Are you sure?"

He said, "Yes, if you want to cross the ditch, this

is a good place." So I pushed the weeds back and forced my way through to the ditch and there in the water was a huge tire from an earth-moving machine lying on its side and spanning the ditch like a bridge. Across I went, once again wondering how he did that.

We then approached a mowed field that had lights on poles around the edge spaced about 100 feet apart.

He said, "Look at your shadows, there are five of them, and imagine that each of them is another person like yourself linked telepathically each to another. Now practice walking across this field, feeling each of them as you walk. See the different views that each of them sees. Feel their bodies. That is a one-star general. Keep walking. Try two stars and finally five. It's a mighty powerful feeling isn't it? Keep walking and let these 'shadows' of you drop behind and below to another reality and behind and below to another and yet another. Keep it up until there are at least five of them, and keep walking in the five different realities at once. Separate but connected. See, you can do it."

I tried it and one shadow walked into a tree, another stumbled on a rock, the whole construct collapsed.

He said, "That's normal, it takes a lot of practice." I tried again and for a short time it worked before it collapsed again. It did feel powerful while it was working! Each time it collapsed though, I felt terrible about the others and eventually I gave up.

Suicide

Finally, after a few more days at my friend's house in Chicago, my brother came to get me away from all this before I either over-dosed or got shot for being an impossible asshole or for yakking too much to some informant. I told him I was just too wired to go to sleep. He told me to just go upstairs and just breathe deeply. I went to bed and tried that for awhile but had no luck. By now I was feeling all sparkly with drugs all the time plus I was concerned not only for my safety but also for the safety of my family on account of the aborted drug deal. I was also immensely embarrassed to discover that most or all of the "powers" I had been wielding were most probably of a community nature and for the most part not "mine". Or, if that wasn't it and I really was so powerful that everything that I said or thought just instantly happened, then I thought I had better stop saying or doing anything in case what I did caused something to go horribly wrong. All trains of thought led to some sort of despair, so I got up to take a walk. As I walked down the road my emotions and mood spiraled farther and farther down, each turn of the spiral reinforced my hopeless state and the conclusion always that it would be best for all for me to die. As I came to a pond I had played in as a child, I decided I should drown myself. I figured I'd swim around in the middle until I was too exhausted and then just sink. I threw myself into the water and discovered that it was only two feet deep. After trying unsuccessfully to breathe the water several times only to choke and sputter, I climbed out and stood on the road. About thirty feet away was an electric pole. I ran as fast as I could and butted the pole with my head. Just before I hit the pole I could see threads of energy going out to my friends and family and to some gurus I had recently met. Then my head hit, I rolled to my right side and watched my left hand right in front of my face clench like a claw while glowing phosphorescent blue and then fading into the already black background.

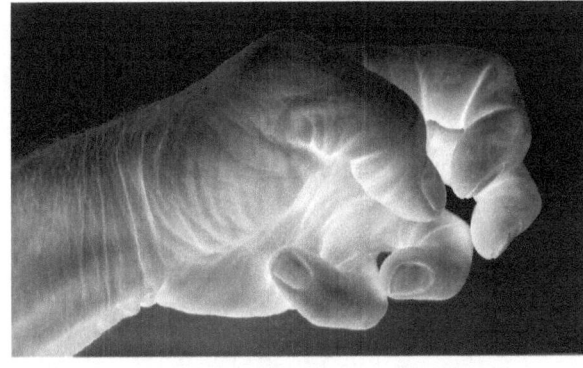

I woke up feeling many of my friends and all of my family tugging on the silver cords. I hurt. I figured I was alive but had no sure way of knowing if that was true. But, whatever, I sure didn't feel like killing myself anymore. I crawled onto the road and stood up, feeling that I had a decision to make as to how I would live out my life extension. I could raise hell against the inequalities of the establishment I had come to dislike intensely. I looked over to the North and imagined I could see a town burning like I had once seen when I was a small child. I seethed. I could see myself waging a small secret war against injustice using my evil for good while killing and burning. I turned about ninety degrees. Now in front of me, out of sight and about 20 miles away was the Bahia Temple. I'd seen it long ago on trips to the lake and thought it very beautiful. Its white purity and complex pattern that looked something like a ninety foot tall three-dimensional paper doily, reminded me of the goodness in people including myself. I stepped forward leaving the hell raiser behind and was awash with relief both from without and within. Everything seemed different, with the road and ground not looking solid, and everything having a sort of sheen of energy or presence.

Sounds were carried in waves. From the far right came the sound of a train whistle, then closer a dog barking, then another bark and closer a bird fluttering and chirping then passing me and on to the left a mouse scampering in the weeds, a bird call, dogs in the distance, and a siren. I could "see" these waves of energy. I was feeling that I must be God or Jesus back again. I was walking through the fields towards the temple and felt as though I was being encouraged to go see if I would be recognized as the new Messiah. With sub-divisions on both sides, these vacant fields seemed to reach all the way to the lake where the temple stood.

I thought, "How could that be?" Again it was decision time.

A sizable spiritual force was in my head, lobbying for picking up the mantle of the new messiah.

"Come on, go for it. The world is in a big mess and needs someone to straighten it out." urged a religious man.

A young woman said. "Get everyone to lie down for one hour all around the world."

"But I don't know how to do that." I answered.

"It doesn't matter. We'll show you as it unfolds. Just have faith." whispered the religious man.

"There have been enough miracles and surely more will happen." The young woman chimed in again.

Another side weighed in with a gravely male voice.

"No way, even if you are The Son of God Himself (which you aren't) they would just kill you like they did Jesus."

"The loony bins are loaded with messiahs. You'd just be another one," said an earnest young man.

"This whole messiah thing is just a way of identifying power-tripping ego maniacs and putting them in their place," another almost shouted. I was convinced.

I veered off the temple path. Now what? I'm not to wreak havoc or teach love. O. K. I'll walk home to Tennessee. What to do about the problems of the world?

"Racism is not as simple as it seems," said a vision of a large black woman. "In order to keep the gene pools necessary for survival we need the different races.

In order to keep the races we need racism. If we eliminate racism we will all turn gray and be wiped out by some virus or something else."

"So, what should we do about the Hitlers and their ilk?" I ask.

"Charismatic megalomaniacs will occasionally arise. They will believe themselves completely and their belief is contagious. Just as people believed the world was flat they will believe these maniacs." Said a sad voice.

I heard screaming and moaning coming from a warehouse. Multiple voices in my head said, "Go, let those people out of there." I can't believe they are really there. But I sit and listen wondering if I should break the door down or call the police. It seems like a mini holocaust. I see visions pasted into my mind from pictures of the holocaust. Like most of the world did before, I finally believe they are not there, and I go on my way. These problems will just have to work themselves out.

Dawn found me wet from head to toe and headed home again. With my fingers I felt that the sides of my scull were broken along those squiggly seams on the sides. I was walking with an odd shuffle. My neck and the top of my spine were feeling all crunched, and some organs felt kind of loose. My friend's brother-in-law stopped on his way to work. He could tell I was not too well, and he took me back to "Mom's" house. I was pretty much not talking to people by then. I could hear what they were saying, but I wasn't quite sure what they meant. Sincerity? Sarcasm? Truth? Lie? Did they mean me? It occurs to me that this could have been what they were talking about in the tower of Babel story. After I was so "high," I just couldn't tell what anyone meant by anything.

When we ate I saw energy coming into the room and watched it concentrate on the food just as someone jabbed their fork into it. It was a perfectly synchronized dance. Except that I couldn't do it. I could see the energy coming, I'd get ready, and by the time I jabbed at it with my fork it was gone, leaving me with "empty" food which I thought was worthless. I used to feel so sure of myself and so smart, now I felt like a dunce. It was obvious to me that everyone had been seeing this energy all of their lives and acting accordingly while I'd been totally blind to it. They looked at me funny or even resentfully as I mimicked their movements in order to actually catch some of the energy-filled food during the brief moments it was on the table.

My brother was concerned about my not talking, and my acting oddly, so he called in a psychiatrist friend to come to the house to take a look at me. At one point in her examination the psychiatrist waved her hand in front of my face to see if my eyes would track it and when they didn't she told my brother and the other onlookers that I'd probably be like a vegetable for the rest of my life. I thought that was silly. She didn't even know I was there. Or maybe she was just trying to rile me up. I'll never know. I think she gave me some pills to take though.

California

My brother took me to California with him. At the airport my toolbox was very heavy and shaped sort of like a casket. I wondered if this was another one of those multiple realities on that big elevator where this time I was accompanying my casket, and I was really dead. But my being dead didn't make sense. If I had died we would be going to Tennessee, not California. It turns out it didn't matter because the box was so heavy we left it behind rather than pay the extra freight to bring it along.

I was really delighted with the plane. It was a 747 and at some point we went up the stairs to the upper deck and I got to look out of the windows. I loved looking at the clouds and the ground so far below and kept looking until my brother said we had to go back down.

We got to my brother's house in Berkeley and energy was flowing everywhere. Waves of energy were flowing across the city and into the room. I felt like I could "see" through the walls. I was taking some sort of tranquilizer, and it really made it hard for me to function. In the morning I would walk down the stairs feeling good and thinking clearly; but, by the time I started eating my cereal, I would feel like someone or some thing was eating my brain with a spoon until I was mostly unable to think.

Little accomplishments were great milestones. When I managed to find my way completely around the block all by myself without going into some other dimension where I feared I might get totally lost, I celebrated the great achievement. The world had become quite different to me. At any given moment there were innumerable directions to be taken. The Euclidean reality I was in could have another approaching at a 45-degree angle that I might step into as it passed. Or a reality would come up from below and I could either step onto and into it and go with it or stay with the one I was in. I could see the disturbances where these "realities" coincided.

Animals would react by jumping or barking or simply rolling over. People would blow their car horns, scratch their heads, turn around or stand up. The world had suddenly acquired a lot more meanings. A small crack in the sidewalk could become next a large crack and then a pot hole followed by a huge crumbling section. I had learned not to go to those places, those side trips, and to stay focused on the more solid sidewalk on my trip around the block.

I was getting a lot better, and was going to group therapy and taking niacin several times a day as an anti-hallucinogen. Still, even though I could find my way around the block, my mind would still take off on any idea and go to the limit or beyond. Or my emotions would fly from happy to scared to angry to meek to strong in a short minute. I broke out the bedroom window on the advice of a poem by my brother-in-law that advised that it was better to break a window than to bash heads or something even more destructive. I still owe my brother for the window. My brother and I would argue for hours about these forces, spirits, waves of energy, and telepathy. He: no, no, no. Me: yes, yes, and yes.

Hitchhiking to Tennessee

I decided it was time to hitchhike to Tennessee. I didn't want to be more of a burden than I was already, so I cut up about half of my clothes and sewed them into a blanket. I packed my belongings for a trip and after borrowing $20 from my brother, I took off south for I-40. Somehow I got over to I-5 headed south. About dark a flat bed truck with stake sides stopped and I got in the back with a young couple and another girl. It was cold so the girl and I cuddled under a blanket and before long we were hot enough for sex. It was a nice ride. We stopped to eat where the road to Tennessee turned left. My social skills in groups were not so good at all so I was, I guess, too quiet and not too forthcoming about myself. The guy who was driving said condescendingly, "Oh, he's one of those." They went on to San Diego, and I turned toward Tennessee.

I thought the next ride was sort of odd because the young man who picked me up said he would be glad to take me all the way to Tennessee. That made me nervous about taking advantage of people, so I said I had changed my mind, and that I had to get off at the next intersection.

The day was absolutely beautiful. I got another ride with some young men who said they were just going to the next intersection but just kept going past more and more of them until I made them let me out. I noticed that they went back in the direction from which they came. I walked over to some trees so I could eat some of the food I had brought with me in the comfort of the shade. A man dressed in ragged clothes like a hobo walked over to me and struck up a conversation. After we talked awhile he said he was a rancher from about 20 miles up the side road. I asked him why he was dressed like a hobo, and he said it was the only way he could get to talk to me. As usual, I didn't know exactly what he meant by that, and also as usual, I declined to ask. The day was so beautiful I

47

started walking along the interstate. For awhile there was an older couple almost walking beside me, I was on the interstate and they were on an access road. Only a fence was separating us. They looked like my uncle and aunt as they smiled and waved and commented on what a nice day it was.

Next was a regular short ride with no offer to take me any farther. I needed something to drink so I walked down the cloverleaf towards a small mini-mart. About halfway around the cloverleaf I met a sun-dried old man and just for the fun of it said, "look at that" and pointed to an irregular stone that had been pushed into the hot pavement. Five minutes later just before I entered the store, I looked back; he was still looking at that spot. I worried about him while I was in the store, and when I came back out, there he was, still looking at that same spot. On the way back up the cloverleaf, I told him it would be all right for him to stop looking at that spot. He said 'OK" and resumed his walk. I didn't ask him if he was just messing with my head.

It was getting dark before I got the next ride, and the man offered to let me sleep at his house. I gratefully accepted his offer. It turned out he only had one bed and wanted me to sleep in it with him which was OK, he didn't try messing with me. Later I got up to get a drink of water and discovered that he had shit in the kitchen sink and on the counters. That was too much, and even though he had been a perfect gentleman, I had to go. After quietly letting myself out, I walked on deep in thought about all that was happening, about my journey, and whether or not I could earn a living when I got back to Tennessee. I was getting very uneasy and absolutely sure that something was very wrong. I stopped thinking long enough to realize that I was lost in thought to the extent that I couldn't even tell where I was or even if I was, as I couldn't even see my body. All I could see with my eyes was a zillion jiggling little different colored splinters of light. After a short panic I decided that gravity should still be working so that if I jumped up and down I should be able to feel my feet hitting the ground. I started jumping and sure enough I began to feel a banging on my feet and began to see them and the little patch of ground I was jumping on. With that as a reference the rest of the picture took shape with the little bits of color rearranging themselves into a world. My knees, waist, more ground, and finally my head and the busy highway I was about to step onto came into view. The realization that I could trust myself even though I was completely preoccupied helped me a great deal.

I wondered if this sort of thing was going on with the spider that I saw walking across the floor during a party. I was sitting on the floor with my head propped against the wall, feeling the swaying of the building, and watching the room full of feet dancing. (About a year later the building rolled down the hill and landed upside down in the street. No one was in it at the time.) A granddaddy long legs spider that was walking across the floor caught my attention. I had noticed before that these spiders were pretty amazing creatures. I did most of my own automobile repair and most of that outside because on the rare occasion when I have had a garage it has been too full to get into. Most any time I'd been working under the hood there was a granddaddy spider or two intently watching my every move as close to the action as possible. So, I'd been wondering if they think about anything. Anyway, here was this spider walking across a floor full of monster human dancers. It went a few paces and changed direction just in time to avoid a deadly squish of a foot then proceeded another foot to stop just in time to let some bare feet pass and so on all at its leisurely pace all the way across the dance floor. Maybe a similar mechanism was at work with the spiders as was with me when I was completely lost in thought.

During the morning rush hour, the next car

stopped. After the usual pleasantries the friendly but earnest fortyish man warned me about how some people didn't like anyone fucking with their minds, and they sure as hell didn't like being moved out of their homes. The tension felt real strong. The guy was being nice to me, just warning me. The next ride took a long time coming. I walked by a sign warning that picking up hitchhikers in the vicinity of a correctional center was dangerous. I walked for a long time to get past the jail, and then had to keep walking past a mining town where a steady stream of cars full of very grim people was passing me as they pulled onto the interstate.

I was lost in thoughts of why these people were angry with me when I came again to a place I had to stop. My vision was again only registering zillions of splinters of light. I jumped up and down and watched as the sphere of my surroundings grew large enough for me to regain my bearings. I was about to step off the edge of a ditch near an overpass. When at last I hitched another ride, the man explained that a hitchhiker had murdered someone earlier that week.

The mine that I had walked past was the largest employer in the town and had been sold to another company. Almost everyone in the town near the plant had to leave that day because they had been evicted from the company-owned housing. No wonder they were grim. He said it was all over a union and management fracas. The next ride I got was with a very clear-headed young man. I don't remember what he said; I just remember that he had the most uncluttered mind of about anyone I'd ever met, and that it was a pleasure to ride with him. After that I got a ride with some young men who said they were going most of the way to Tennessee, but they had to check their transmission first. I was a little worried about a couple of things, first, was I being "handled" and second if not the other first, was I mentally influencing them. While the car was being checked out I went to a mini mart and bought a six pack. We were sitting by a wall talking and the driver asked me if I wanted to go to the "farm" up in Washington. I said, no I had a farm in Tennessee that I was heading for. He said, it had damn well better be there and that he was getting damn tired of sitting on a cactus when he talked to me, whereupon I also discovered that I was sitting on some cactus. By the time the car was ready, I had become convinced that they were handling me and decided not to go with them.

I was getting pretty far into the desert by now and nobody had picked me up for quite some time so I was walking. I walked until sometime after dark then rolled up into my blanket and went to sleep. The next morning I woke up and started walking again and saw in the distance what looked like an old man walking the same direction as I was. I thought I would overtake him in a short time and strike up a conversation with him. I hadn't talked to anyone since the previous afternoon so I was feeling pretty "out there." Of course my thoughts would frequently turn to the task of trying to come up with a scenario, hypothesis, or theory that would account for all the things that were happening to me. For awhile it was kind of ego boosting to feel like I was a God, but that turned into solipsism, and it soon got to be just too lonely. I began to think that I was thinking about everything just after it happened instead of just before it happened. If that was the case then I was only reacting and wasn't thinking anything original. While these thoughts were roiling within, and I was feeling sorry for myself, I saw a discarded hypodermic needle and put it in my pack.

I got close enough to the man in front of me to see him look back. I guess he didn't like what he saw so he put on a steady slightly faster pace than mine and in a few hours he had simply walked away. One of the reasons I wanted to talk to the old man is that he looked sort of like a hermit I had met who lived in the desert ever since he had come back from World War II. I thought if this man was like that man, he would have some advice for me.

I was approaching a crossroads and by now was nearly out of money and hadn't even gotten out of California. On the way down the long hill to the crossroad community of a couple of houses, a small grocery store and gas station, I decided that I too could live in the desert like a hobo for the rest of my life. The mountains in the distance looked kind of purple and all in all it was a really beautiful place to live. So, after crossing the crossroads I veered left off the road and into the desert. After going about a mile into the desert, while I was hiking up a gentle slope, a couple of jets roared overhead and it sounded like they blew up the other side of the hill. They were probably breaking the sound barrier because even in a firing range they wouldn't do that all that close to the houses, but I didn't know that for sure so I veered off toward the mountains. While worrying about how I was going to get some water, I saw about three turtles lying in the sand under a Joshua tree. Hmm, I thought, I could drink their blood and a clear image of me drinking blood from them as if they were canteens came to mind. They all lifted their heads and hissed at me. Obviously upset. I looked at them. They looked at me. And I decided to just go back to civilization. Just a short time after that I almost stepped on a small rattlesnake that jumped up on its tail and skittered backwards scared shitless. Its fear was contagious and I began to look for scorpions, rattlesnakes and Gila monsters everywhere. It occurred to me that my deep sleep the night before might have been a bit naive.

My stay in the desert having ended, I once again started to hitchhike or at least started to stick my thumb out. The cars were not easily stopped and I began to look on the scrap computer printouts that my brother had given me to write notes on to see if they said anything about not leaving California after all. If I was being "handled," maybe these had something to do with it. They didn't make much sense to me but none of them mentioned any area outside California. This was logical since they were scrap paper from his job at the Planning Commission. At any rate I couldn't get a ride toward Tennessee so I thought I'd try going north first then turning east. After some time, I decided that wasn't working either, so I turned south which didn't work and then began trying any way a car was coming. Whenever I saw a car coming I would jump to the appropriate side of the road to thumb a ride. Eventually I did get a ride, going back the way I had come.

Catching a Freight Train

For awhile the road into Bakersfield travels alongside the railroad and occasionally I would see a train overtake us or vice versa, and it got me thinking of some of the stories that Dad would tell about hoboing around during the great depression. When my ride ended, I got out where a railroad yard was adjacent to the road. More and more I was feeling as though I was being "handled" and that I could do pretty much anything that I wanted. So, I decided to hop a freight car going north. I went over to the track that had a train that was moving back and forth every so often and waited for it to start making its move north. Pretty soon it was moving about five or six miles an hour and I clambered into an empty boxcar. About 200 yards later the train stopped so I got out and waited a bit longer. Here came a guy with a backpack saying he'd seen me get on and off and was going to catch a train too. I asked him how you know how to catch a train that is going in the direction you want to go. He said it was simple, you just ask the engineer where he is going and they tell you and then you ask them if they will let you ride and most of the time they say sure.

We had climbed up on a flat car to talk and in the brighter light I noticed that this guy was very clean for a guy who was riding freight cars so I began to mistrust him. While we were talking, the train next to us was picking up speed, now up to about 10 miles per hour, and in mid-sentence I jumped from the flatcar into a boxcar. The train kept increasing its speed and I realized that I was indeed on a freight train ride. Until the train left the freight yard I tried to stay out of the light. Soon we were out in the city and then moving into the countryside and hurtling down the track swaying from side to side.

At first it was terrifying, but I decided to trust the engineer, put the thoughts of dying in a train wreck out of my mind, and fall into a fitful sleep. I awoke when things began to calm down and realized that the train was probably going to stop. It did and I sat in the car for a bit because I didn't know if it was going to start up again. Suddenly there was a loud BAM BAM BA BAMz accompanied by the words in my head, GET OFF THE TRAIN! I thought someone had shot at the car I was in or hit it with a sledgehammer. I looked out both sides and didn't see anyone so I slipped out of the train and walked toward the engine. I toyed with the thought of asking the engineer for a ride and such but when I reached the engine I found it was probably not possible. The engine had stopped at an intersection with a road. A broken train gate was laying in the middle of the crossing and a small brick building with a light on was right beside the track. I didn't go inside the engine or the little building but I couldn't see anyone anywhere outside or by looking through the windows, so I walked toward the city light into, I think, Fresno looking for a place to sleep.

Suicide Again

By now I was crazy as a loon, out of money and probably not able to earn any anywhere doing anything. More and more I walked down that spiral path into that pit of depression until I decided once again that I should just kill myself. I noticed a radio tower with a little thicket of sumac or some fifteen-foot tall shrub at its base and decided that would be a good place. This time I took out the pills I had for tranquilizing and for anti-hallucinating and I chewed them up, mixed them with water, and shot some into my arm and swallowed the rest. And lay me down to sleep.

Crazy Men

Once again the Lord didn't take my soul. I woke up in the night, staggered to the street and flagged down the first car I saw, telling the Hispanic trio that they had to take me to the hospital because I was crazy and needed help. That sometimes I thought I was God, sometimes I thought I was a clam, and sometimes I thought I didn't even think, but that I was only reacting to what was around me. So, right now I needed to go to the hospital. They said get in we'll take you, but first we have to get something to eat. A short time later we pulled into a drive-in or drive-thru restaurant and the guy driving pulled out his gun pointed it at the waitress and ordered hamburgers and fries. I said I wasn't hungry. Surely they knew the waitress, but I didn't see them pay.

They weren't in any hurry, so I said, "Come on, I have to get to the hospital, I'm crazy and have to deal with it."

They said, "Yeah, we'll get you there we know where it is," and then lit up a joint and passed it around.

After a few turns I reminded them again and they said they were getting closer. Then they saw a middle-aged woman driving a white Cadillac in front of them and pulled up beside it hollering that they were horny and wanted to fuck her and after swerving close to her fender a couple of times they drove her car right up on the sidewalk.

I started screaming. "FOR GOD SAKE QUIT THAT, I'M THE CRAZY ONE AROUND HERE, AND YOU ARE SUPPOSED TO BE TAKING ME TO THE DAMNED HOSPITAL."

They said, "O. K. we are almost there."

Sure enough, after about two blocks we pulled into the parking lot.

I thanked them for the ride and headed for the front entrance. When I got to the door a nurse was holding

57

the door open while a male nurse was pushing a Harley Hog into the hospital. I wondered if I'd come to a fancy garage instead of a hospital and asked them what was wrong with their patient. They looked at me suspiciously and didn't answer. When I first entered the admission room I didn't see anyone at all. The room was quite large and filled with waiting chairs. To one side there was a counter segmented by little Formica walls every two feet. About two thirds of the way down I spotted an elderly woman doing a crossword puzzle.

I went over to her, and she asked, "Can I help you?"

"Yes." I said. "I'm crazy and need to commit myself."

Handing me a sheaf of papers she said, "Here, fill these out."

"I don't have any money." I admitted.

"That doesn't matter 'cause the paperwork won't come back for two weeks and by then you'll be out of here." She explained with a knowing smile.

While I was filling out the papers the dawn was slowly breaking, and in comparison to all these other people I was feeling pretty sane.

I took the papers up to the lady and said, "Just put these somewhere while I think about this. I may be back in a few hours."

"O. K., I'll keep them under the desk here, but I don't come in to work until eleven in the evening. Good luck."

I said, "Great. Thank you."

I walked out into the breaking dawn. By now I was very hungry and as I started walking out of town on a four-lane road I noticed not manna from heaven but almonds from semis. They must grow a lot of them along there and haul them by the heaping trucks full because about every couple of feet along the side of the road was a delicious almond. I got another ride, this time not very far. As we rode along we talked about the Pacific Ocean and how nice it was over there, and I began to think I should go in that direction.

Earning Money

I was concerned about running out of money and had resigned myself to going back to my brother's house, but really didn't want to be a big drain on my family. I was dropped off on the outskirts of a small town and at the intersection was a small drive-in diner. There was trash all over the parking lot and it just looked terrible. Other than the mess, the place was very nice. As a child, I was concerned about the Bible's, "If your eye offends you, pluck it out." Rather than take it literally, so I would have to pluck my eyes out, I decided it meant, at least in the case of litter, that if litter offends you, just pick it up and get it out of your eye's sight. A lot better, I thought, than having a bunch of blind people running around a dirty parking lot bleeding from their eye holes. So, I began to pick up the litter. I was sorting pop-tops into one pile, old flattened straws in another, aluminum cans in another and so forth.

After about 30 or 40 minutes of this a manager came out from inside and asked, "What are you doing?"

I said, "I'm just picking up this trash around the parking lot because it looks so bad it makes my eyes hurt."

He looked around the lot, seemed to digest that for awhile, and asked, "Would it help if I let you use a rake?"

"Oh, yes." I said, and with the rake, continued cleaning the parking lot with new-found energy.

When I was done I ended up just dumping my carefully sorted piles into the same trash can. I returned the rake and the manager said, "You were right, that looks a lot better." And after handing me two dollars, said, "Here, this isn't much, but I really appreciate your opening my eyes."

I could make a living! I could survive after all. A warm glow surrounded me; I was very pleased.

Kindred Soul

At the next intersection I bought a coke at a gas station with my new money and instead of getting on the interstate and heading north towards my brother's house, I headed west to visit the ocean. I was still hungry and noticed a bag from a hamburger joint lying in the grass. I looked in the bag hoping for something to eat and discovered half of a hamburger and was delighted until just before I got it to my mouth I saw that the meat was almost obscured by crawling ants. Still, I looked at it and thought about the protein in insects and that I really was hungry and had it not been for the almonds along the road, I would have given it a try. Instead, I tossed it down thinking, not yet. After I had gone west for about a mile or two, I saw a barn-sized pile of hay bales and beyond it on a hill in the same field, a ramshackle house? Shack? Lean to? It looked pretty jumbled and a lot like my home in Tennessee, so I headed across the field towards it hoping to find a place of respite and a kindred soul. When I got to within 50 feet of the door, which was really a missing wall, an elderly black man came out and walked toward me.

He looked me over and muttered mostly to himself, "It was a long time ago, but they still keep coming."

I said, "I saw your house from the road and it looked and felt so much like my home in Tennessee that I had to come see if anyone was home. I think that I've gone crazy because I see all this energy coursing around and lots of the time it makes what ever people say mean a lot of different things so I'm almost always confused."

He said, "I guess you are hungry. Come on in and have some dinner."

By the time we had finished dinner, which was something from a can, it had gotten dark. We sat and listened to a small radio.

I would see energy coming and when it got to us he would, depending on how the energy wave went say, "Emmhmmm" or, "emm emmhmmmm" or, "hmmmmhmmmm."

It was very very nice and comfortable to feel that someone else in the world could see and feel this energy just like I could and be able to acknowledge it. Unlike most of the rest of the people who though they acted and reacted with this energy like pros, refused to admit it's existence. The next morning he went off to do some work. While he was gone I tried to clean up his kitchen and after much scrubbing discovered that his little two-burner gas stove was white porcelain. The roof had some pretty large holes and gaps in the tin so I climbed up on it and was repairing it when he came back. In no uncertain terms he demanded that I come down from there. After protesting, I climbed down. He seemed relieved that I hadn't gotten hurt, and though I explained to him that I was a carpenter and climbing on things just wasn't dangerous for me, he said he just didn't want to take any chances. I thanked him profusely for letting me stay for awhile. He said I was welcome to stay as long as I needed a place, and I thought he meant it.

After that visit I was a lot stronger and didn't feel quite so crazy. Since I had figured out that I could make a living after all, I decided I could go back to my brother's house to borrow some money and just fly home. I walked back to the interstate and pretty soon caught another ride, this time with a nicely dressed salesman on his way home after being on the road for a week.

We didn't talk very much, but I remember that just before he let me out he asked in a questioning manner, "You're him, aren't you?"

"Who?" I wondered.

"The hitch hiker everyone back down the road has been talking about."

"You aren't talking about the one who killed someone are you?"

"No." He said. "The people in the stores I called on back down the road were talking about a hitchhiker who looked like you. They said there were some pretty amazing mental happenings going on back there."

"Yeah, I think that might have been me." I admitted.

By the time I caught another ride it was dark and I was turning toward Berkeley. A motor home with a couple on their way to San Francisco picked me up. They let me out just a few blocks from my brother's house. As I crossed Shattuck while walking up the gentle hill in Berkeley I thought that though I hadn't made it to Tennessee I'd gotten a lot further this time than I had when I managed to make it around the block.

I had called my brother to ask him if I could come back and of course he said yes, so he and his wife weren't totally surprised when I knocked on the door. His telephone number was and continues to be the only one I ever was able to remember regardless of what state, country, or universe my mind was in. In the day or two it took to get on a flight, I got more pills and more niacin to keep me a bit calmed down. I told my brother and his wife about some of my adventures and how nice and helpful it was to spend that time with the black man at his shack. They tried to look him up when they got over that way about a month later, but couldn't find him. The plan was for me to take the red eye back to Chicago, then pick up my toolbox and ride with my friends back to Tennessee.

I got on the plane and my arm, which had been starting to hurt and swell up where I had injected it full of crap, began to throb with excruciating pain. I guess there was a difference in air pressure or maybe it was just getting worse. I asked the flight attendant to bring me some Tylenol and just hung on until we landed. I had never felt so much pain and discomfort. Being in a confined space made it impossible for me to get the pain out of my mind. I knew I couldn't go to my friend's house in that condition so I called them and told them I was going downtown and would be there after they got home from work. I was in such a painful cloud that I don't remember whether I took a bus or a train down town to the big hospital. I do remember how relieved I was when I finally saw it across the street. The hospital was mobbed with people with all sorts of maladies, and after what seemed like three weeks of sitting there enclosed in my ball of pain, my name was called.

I went inside an examining room and waited again. On the other side of a sheet was an elderly black woman who was there to get her ingrown toenails cut out. The doctor cut on her first and she was screaming and whimpering and carrying on. When the doctor was done and had gotten to me, I asked him if he hadn't given her any Novocain. He said no, the policy was that if they made it a pleasant experience for patients at the hospital, they would come back for every little thing instead of just the important stuff. It didn't matter to me if I had Novocain or not because my arm already hurt as much as it could, but that policy seemed pretty harsh to me. The doctor asked me what had happened. I told him I had found a syringe in the desert and figured it had been in the sun long enough to be sterilized and had used it to attempt suicide but apparently had either missed my vein or had gone through it. He said, "Well, you must be smarter than

65

you look." Then he lanced the abscess, squeezed some stinking pus out of it and stuffed some Betadine soaked gauze back into the hole.

I took the bus up to my friend's house and got there about dark. They seemed glad to see me again, but I certainly wouldn't have been surprised if they weren't all that happy. The next morning my friend took me back to Tennessee. The car had a very nice stereo and the trip was very mellow and pleasant.

Back in Tennessee

I was taken aback to find that in my absence my parents had moved into a funeral home. It hadn't been one for quite awhile, but when I was in high school I went to school with the son of the owner and their house was in the same building as the funeral home. It took some time to convince myself that I hadn't died and gone to some strange afterlife where my family was visiting my body in the funeral home while I didn't know I had died. Was this another "elevator reality?" I decided it wasn't. Being home was different. For awhile I lived in the funeral-home-turned-boarding-house with my mother, sometimes my father, and an older lady, the manager.

A young woman lived there sometimes too, and I enjoyed her company, especially when she decided to seduce me. Apparently she was pretty crazy because she spent all her money on visits to a shrink. We talked about being crazy and what was involved with all that, and even though she seduced me a time or two, we were mainly friends. One day a young man who was working on his doctoral thesis came from the university to interview me about some of my odd experiences. We went out to the river to talk and then jumped across onto a large rock to continue talking. While we were talking I got the feeling that he felt superior to me and that he was skeptical of some of the things I was saying, so when we were through, I jumped back across first and then when I felt he was in mid-air jumping, I sent him a mighty strong mental "push." Well, he fell into the river and lost his glasses in the swift water. I felt bad about him losing his glasses and helped him get them from the river bottom. With my glasses still on, I could see them, and with my slightly longer reach I was able to grab them.

I told my lady friend this story and she got all excited and said, "So you 'pushed' him into the river?"

I said, "He could have just slipped."

"But, you lured him out there onto that rock into a situation where he was insecure enough to fall into the river and lose his glasses, and then you got his glasses back for him?"

"I had just thought it would be a nice place to talk in a relaxing manner." I said.

She was real good for my ego.

I thought part of the deal was that I had to go to a shrink, so I started going to one. He didn't order a physical for me and I didn't tell him that my head had been cracked so he assumed that drugs had caused my problem and told me I had to quit cold turkey. This was not very hard to do because I hadn't had any drugs of any kind for at least a month. When I told him about hearing voices, seeing fields of energy, and everything not really seeming to be solid anymore, he said that those were symptoms of schizophrenia. Then he explained that he thought that the communication link between the two halves of my brain had been somehow blocked or severed so they could no longer function as a unit. I still waffled between having some unique abilities and being the only one who wasn't already used to having and using these abilities.

Back to my House

When spring came and it wasn't such a bother to keep my house warm, I moved back to my own house. My builder friend was about to finish the house I had worked on and he asked me to make a custom front door for it. This was really nice of him because I wasn't making much of a living doing my artwork. I tried to build things while working on them in both the "real" world and in the "psychic" world. This of course made it a lot harder to build things. My thoughts were very hard to control. At almost any moment my thought process could go completely out of control and expand like an explosion until I had to lie down on the bed, dig my hands and feet into my covers and hang on until things calmed down. My brain would get so busy that it was like being in the center of a great white light of activity. I found that after about fifteen or twenty minutes of white light, things would get back to normal and I could function in my "normal" fashion for awhile. I began to see this as the sloshing of liquid in a tank and decided to install baffles to slow down my thinking process. Different key words would invoke koans or riddles as permeable barriers stretched across my thought tank to impede any runaway thought processes. This started to bring some stability into my thought world. It made me think a lot slower but still sped up the thought process by eliminating a lot of unnecessary and extreme indecision.

I couldn't find things anymore. I had to backtrack as if I was going backward through time just to find things like my coffee cup or pencil or a tool I had just been using. I remember reading about this problem in an article about computer vision. If the angle of the view changed, the object didn't look the same and was unrecognizable to the computer. This problem used to be handled by my unconscious mind. Apparently my unconscious automatically kept an updated map of the general vicinity so I could go directly to my pencil or cup without backtracking, but now I was in manual mode. I figured that all I had to do was to build an automatic transmission. My subconscious was already beating my heart, breathing and digesting food so I knew it was still working. I just needed to tell it to map the area and take care of these other things it had forgotten about. So, I looked at everything in the room from each direction, and then scanned crosswise and finally everything seemed to have a place. Sure enough, after about a week of mapping my surroundings at least twice every day, I could find things without backtracking.

More and more I was feeling as if other entities were taking control of my body. I passively watched how they did it and thought I was slowly learning how to do it myself. Unfortunately, during this watching I was getting farther and farther from my body. After about two weeks I was about ten feet from it, looking at it through a shimmering haze of psychic activity. I was so weak psychically that my two dogs decided that they were stronger than I was and they threatened to tear me apart, each of them biting harder and harder, one on my left hand and one on my right hand. I summoned up enough strength to make them believe I could still do them incredible harm, so they let me go, but it was very scary for me and sort of a wake-up call. I decided it was time to get back into my body. First I went the short distance to God and asked if it was all right if I went back to my body because I had some unfinished business to attend to. God laughed and said sure go ahead. So now when an entity entered my body, instead of meekly letting it do what it willed, I gripped it with my mind and marched it to my own tune. One day while driving my mother around, I linked with her mind and made a mental "tape" of us backing up. We backed up for about a half-mile while I "recorded" this "tape" into my memory. Later while I was driving, a familiar but bothersome entity came into my body. I grabbed it and while I was driving forward I played the tape from my memory with the entity backing up. I was getting much stronger.

I had been worried Zen-like about the worms in the garden and if these layers of reality like the layers of an onion could be viewed such that the fighting ants really did represent one for one a fight that was going on somewhere else in the world. Later, I plunged my shovel into the ground just outside my kitchen window and at that very second the radio newscaster broke into the program with the news that there had been an earthquake in Chile. Kind of freaky, but I kept digging.

I was worried that my car might not make the trip to town one day, so before I left I checked out the oil, the gas, the water and the air in the tires. During the twenty-mile trip into town I passed about five cars with their hoods up or with a flat tire.

One day, I got very fearful that someone was going to come to do me harm. Later that day I went out to the store and found that the county road department had dug a ditch across the road to replace a culvert. I turned around to go out the other way and came to a ditch being dug across the road there too. I just turned around and went back home.

The next day a friend of mine came to visit, found me in my yard and said, "Steven, you have got to stop. You are literally raising hell." I shrugged.

Another friend came out to tell me "You son of a bitch, you made me back up for a half mile the other day."

I grinned.

Cooking Up a Beautiful Day

I felt strong enough that I could take it a little easier now so I started to clean my kitchen. Soon after I started, a really nice older lady entered my body and said, "No, not that way." And then she proceeded to give me a lesson in which type of Mason jar is meant to hold which kinds of food. I think the flour went into the Atlas jar, the raisins and fruit into the Ball jar, Kerr got pasta and Star got the sugar. Or something like that. After everything was in its rightful place then the alchemical cookery began. For biscuits she started with the Atlas flour to hold the earth then added the Star baking soda to fertilize it then Kerr milk added moisture and Ball salt seasoned it and I forget what kind of butter made it taste so good. Then into the oven it went, so the sun would shine on it, and ta da, what a beautiful way to start a beautiful day. And boy howdy, did she ever cook up a beautiful day.

Transparency

My life seemed totally transparent. When I went to town, after working on a belt ornament the night before, a friend grabbed her belt right where the ornament I had been working on would go and wiggled her eyebrows meaningfully. It seemed as though everyone knew what I was doing, but I didn't have a clue about anything they had been doing. So, once again I felt left out, as if I was the only one who wasn't telepathic or who was only recently telepathic while everyone else had been doing it all their lives. I decided that people who came over could determine too much about what I had been doing just by reading the titles of the books I'd been reading, so I put gray jackets over a bunch of them. I put them upstairs, and then screamed in my mind, I'm not letting anyone up my stairs anymore. Fifteen minutes later, a good friend arrived with some people I'd never met.

I let them in, and the first thing my friend said was, "Can I show these people the upstairs?"

I just resigned myself and said, "Sure."

My friend the builder came to pick up the door that I had finished. One night while he was there, some other friends came over, and the four of us sat around the fireplace smoking pot. I didn't need any because I still hadn't come down enough for it to make any difference. We began channeling some powerful entities that were coming and going with sparks from the fire and creaks from the house. They reminded me of the five-star generals in the field of lights.

At one point one of them channeled in and asked another "What are we all doing here?" The reply was a nod of his head in my direction.

The "newcomer" said, "Oh, I see."

I'm not sure what he saw, but after awhile he left and we all went to bed. My friend took off with the door the next morning.

73

Electrical Problems and Flying Exam

My electricity got turned off because I was late paying my bill. I was pretty sore about this and complained to them asking them why it was that other people could be late for months without getting their electricity turned off but not me. They said it was because I had been late before some years in the past.

I was still mad about it when I went to West Knoxville for a visit with some friends. There, while walking along the railroad track, I found a beautiful orange pipe about the length of my VW and 4" in diameter. I strapped this to the top of my car and because I thought maybe I was stealing it, I drove in a long circuitous route back to my house. Earlier I had gotten a gift of some large diameter copper wire from the wife of a man who had died. She thought I could use it to make some sculpture.

That night, I was supposed to be studying for the written test for my student pilot license. It was to take place at the airport at 9:00 in the morning. My airplane instructor had told me about a problem with the electric company about moving the large power line from the end of the runway so that the runway could be extended. I thought the orange pipe would make a pretty good insulation and there was enough of the copper wire to cut into pieces, weld together and stuff into the ends of the pipe to make it look like a big piece of wire representing the runway's missing link. All the while I was working; I was channeling energy from the airport argument combining it with the recent passing of the friend of the family, and my own considerable energy.

I was working by the light of kerosene and Coleman lamps. I worried that this sculpture wasn't good enough to warrant the use of the copper wire gift but decided to use it anyway. Soon I had an awesome arched piece of insulated wire. It definitely looked like a piece of electric company wire. I briefly wondered just who those people were who had come to me saying that they were ready to blow up the transmission lines in the area and wondered again why they thought I might want them to.

I had said "Oh, heavens no. We don't want to go to war."

My sister had sent me a vest that she had sewn herself. It was pretty new but I decided it would look good on the wire if I just added a hook so it would look like a giant coat hanger. I found a piece of 3/4 inch gas pipe about eight feet long that would do fine for piercing the wire. As I was welding a pad on the bottom of the hook so it wouldn't go all the way through the wire, I began to mumble to myself about what a good fishing hook it would make.

I imagined I was some electrical worker just waking up from a sound sleep and began to say to myself that it would be a fine day to go fishing in the morning. As a matter of fact I could just go over to that switch and flip it off and fish for about an hour while they called me to go investigate the trouble. Then after catching a couple of big ones I could just go back to the switch and flip it on and report that some squirrel must have flipped a breaker.

Just at daybreak I was finished with the sculpture, a gigantic coat hanger with a regular size vest on it. It was overflowing with symbolism. So, I taped my electric bill to it and dropped it off at the electric company on my way to the FAA office to take the written exam for my student flying license.

When I walked into the FAA office, the Flight Service Station I believe it was called, I saw that the clock said 8:00. My appointment was for nine so I sat down and grabbed a magazine for the hour-long wait.

A man came from the other room and asked me, "Can I help you?"

"Not really." I said, pointing at the clock. "I'm here for my student license exam, but I guess I'm an hour early."

He looked at me a bit oddly and said "OK, just wait here."

I sat down and had no sooner gotten settled in for the hour's wait when the same man came into the room carrying a chair. He put the chair down, climbed up on it and set the clock forward to a few minutes after nine and then after climbing down, he picked up the chair and went back into the other room.

Poking his head back through the door he said, "You can come in now. The power has been off for the past hour and it came back on just before you walked in."

I took my exam and passed it. I think they sent me the results later with my student license. I drove back home wondering if that electric worker I was imagining had indeed gone fishing. After I took a much needed nap and did some relaxing around the house, some friends of mine dropped in. They were particularly interested in what I had done last night. At first I told them I had been studying, then that I had been working on a sculpture, a sort of response to having my electricity turned off, then that I had been thinking a lot last night about going fishing for an hour this morning. And that the power had been off at the Flight Service Station just before I had gotten there. And suddenly one of them said, "Oh, my God! I know what he did! Let's go!" Then they drove away in a hurry.

I drove into Gatlinburg in the afternoon and could have sworn I saw the sculpture hanging on a pole by the electric company. When I checked the next day it wasn't there. Maybe I imagined it.

Another time when I was thinking about flying I saw a moth sitting on the edge of the bookshelf. It was mostly being still, just occasionally fluttering its wings. Was it perhaps meditating? Suddenly it took off and after an erratic zigzag flight it landed on the back of a chair. There it sat for awhile until again after an incredibly complex flight it landed on the desk. After a rest it took off on an attack at the light bulb followed by another rest or meditation then another attack, again and again, then after due consideration, another erratic zigzag back to the bookshelf. I think it was sitting there thinking, "I want to fly to the desk so I can better assault the bright light. So, I fly straight at it for two inches then straight up for one half inch then left for a third of a second and arc back to the right and up for three inches then a complete flip so I can see if I'm being followed... (etc.)...then a three-inch arc down and to the left to a landing on the desk." For something with such a small brain it would take awhile to figure out a flight plan like that.

Time Travel

As a student pilot I had to know my right from my left and I had some trouble with that, so I painted my little fingernails red on the left hand and green on the right hand, and pretended that I was an airplane with my marker lights glowing. As I mentioned before I imagined I was flying when I was driving a car. Ever since that "Eat that bite" episode where I slipped through the back of my chair and experienced that disassociation from my body I felt that I was flying when I was moving. Sometimes I would fly with 'reality,' sometimes parallel to it, or sometimes nowhere near it. One day when I was running late for some appointment, it occurred to me that I might be able to take a shortcut through that disassociated type space. I was driving in the car about 25 miles from Gatlinburg and decided that I could make a straight line to Gatlinburg through the hills and everything and pretend that that was 'reality' and that the car on the road was the disassociated reality. This took lots of concentration. I really didn't want to lose concentration on what was happening on the real road. When I got to my appointment in Gatlinburg, I was still about twenty minutes late. I was disappointed that I hadn't made up any time, but was pleasantly surprised to find out that I had gotten there before the people I was supposed to meet. On other days when I tried to do this it worked similarly. The people I was supposed to meet were always as late as or later than I was.

Back then women liked me a lot. I considered that fortunate because the feeling was returned; though in retrospect I probably would have gotten a lot more work done if they hadn't liked me. Anyway this was in the land before AIDS, and STDs that could kill you, and many people enjoyed "free love" including me. After some time, I began to regularly date about four different women. They all knew this and took it in stride as did I when I thought about them and their "others".

One week I began to fantasize about time travel and thought it would be pretty neat if we could travel through time while making love. I would disassociate or leave my/our bodies and fly through time and space, twisting and turning, expanding and shrinking and stretching and loving, oh my! Well, in the midst of it all she started her period. This was OK with me but I couldn't help wondering if maybe all that travel through time had reset her biological clock. A day or so later I was making love with another girlfriend, soaring through time and all and she too started to menstruate. I wondered anew if this pseudo time travel had somehow triggered her "clock". Another day, another woman hurtling through space-time with me, another period started. I've heard that women who live together can get on the same schedule but these women didn't live together and they each said they were surprised they started so early. Anyway, I quit sexual time travel fantasy but I still wonder what was going on or if it was just coincidence. Being shy about those things, I never did ask what the woman's experience was.

I still think it is possible to do some sort of time travel, perhaps studying why some days seem so much longer than others could lend a clue. I just don't know how yet. I don't even know how to determine if one day really is or is not longer than another. Thoughts like that used to send me off to the great white light, but now I can stop and let them remain unresolved. Or I can just file them as silly.

DNA Halo

One night while driving to Gatlinburg a pair of glowing lights like the lit ends of the sparklers used on July Fourth appeared in my third eye space. They rotated like a golden sparkling double helix as they burned their way around my mind and head. It was almost as if I was forcibly getting married to some entity. Or was I being enslaved with a telepathic mind control device? It reminded me of the scooping out of my mind while I was eating my cereal in the morning back in California. Or, of the feeling I got in the morning after my first puff of a cigarette when I felt like manacles were clamped onto my mind, locking my mind with a bunch of other minds. But, maybe it wasn't quite so sinister or malevolent. Perhaps even helpful and beneficent like the entity that bet me I wouldn't be able to see anyone for an hour. Maybe I could learn to use it. I just couldn't be sure. Sometimes I had the feeling that it was there to prevent me from further screwing things up in the universe. That part sounded good. But it was definitely some type of mind control. Was it a filter of some kind? Why then wasn't it in the shape of a colander? I did know that if this was a halo, no one in or out of a body had asked me if I wanted it; it sure wasn't any merit badge. Whatever it was, it represented some real and powerful force.

Building Doors

It was time to do another door. This door was really a double door that opened in the middle, and it had to be quite sturdy. My father had been a carpenter, so I asked him to assist me with building the basic door to which I would then add the metal panels.

We took up this task in the warehouse where he was building his Ferro-Cement boat. We took some old rough sawn timbers he had gotten for holding the mesh for his boat together until the cement was added and after re-sawing them, we started to lay them out on the floor.

He showed me how to make some of the pieces represent pieces of the psychic "firmament" and how to align those with the cardinal directions and then affix them with the proper cross pieces so they would channel any spirits or other people's thoughts such that they couldn't pass through unless the door was open.

I had read about the Bermuda triangle ever since I was in high school and lately had been thinking that some of those effects could be similar to the different realities I had been experiencing. One of the four metal panels had an abstract picture of the ocean being sectioned by different realities. This was very subtle. Different realities in the great expanse of the ocean can look pretty much the same. This view illustrated just how difficult it can be to find ones way in an area of converging universes.

If I remember correctly, this panel also contained a little piece of double helix that represented the burning of the glowing golden double helix around my mind that night. I've seen other artworks with little snippets of golden double helix and suspect that those artists have also experienced a similar vision.

I finished the doors and loaded them into my station wagon to drive to Chicago. About half way to Chicago I saw a young man lying beside the road with his body arched back over his duffel bag or back pack, his legs toward the oncoming traffic, and his head out of sight behind the bag. Except for his arm holding up his hand in a thumbing gesture I couldn't tell if he was asleep or awake. It was such a novel way to hitchhike that I had to pick him up. It took me about a hundred yards to stop and as I backed toward him he stood up.

"Thanks for stopping." he said, "I thought I would be there forever."

"No problem. Throw your pack in the back seat. I've never seen anyone try to get a ride by lying backwards over his pack on the side of the road before. I just had to stop."

"I was getting real tired and hot and depressed." he said. "How far are you going?"

"A little past Chicago," I told him. "How about you?"

"That's great. I'm going to Chicago to visit friends."

"You look kind of Indian." I said, "Where you from?"

"I'm a Navaho, born on the reservation," he said proudly.

"That's cool. I'm Steve; I guess we're going to Chicago."

"All right, I'm Bear," he said, sticking out his hand.

"Good to meet you," I shook his hand. "Hey, I'm going out west to meet my girlfriend soon. She and a friend of hers are helping to tend sheep on a Navaho ranch. Anything I need to know?"

"Watch out for the Scorpions," he said seriously.

"And rattlesnakes?" I asked.

"No", he said, "These scorpions are a loosely organized gang of young Navaho men who will come to ask you for a fee for whatever you might be doing on the reservation." Then he added, "When they come to ask for money, it is absolutely necessary to treat them with respect."

"I don't usually have much money." I said, "How much do they usually ask for?"

"It isn't really all that bad." He said, "It's customary to haggle over the price. You've got to ask them to lower the price. But, after they lower the price three times, you have to accept it, because to be asked to lower the price any more than three times is considered very insulting."

"O K, lower three times. With respect. Anything else?" I asked.

"Oh, yes," he added. "Don't pay for anything with a twenty-dollar bill. Indians don't like Andrew Jackson. His picture reminds them of the white man raping their women, killing their kids and stealing their land. If they're a little drunk, they'll blame it all on you."

"O K, ditch the twenties." I added to my list. "What about peyote?" I wondered aloud. "Can I get some while I'm there?"

"The Indians of the Pentecostal church use it in their vision quests. But they won't sell you any," he said.

"Surely there's a way?" I hoped.

"The only way you can get peyote from the Indians is to first ask to buy some wine on the reservation and then follow the instructions they give you. But remember it is very important to ask them for the wine to be in quart bottles, not in fifths."

He got out somewhere on the outskirts of Chicago and I went on to deliver the doors. I didn't stay very long in Chicago this time but when I delivered the doors the guys were using the first door I'd made as a coffee table. Apparently the person who had bought the house had said "I'll buy this house if you will take that damn door off."

A bit hard on the ego, but still, the door had been instrumental in the sale of the house, and after all, that was its purpose. While we sat around I took the opportunity to ask if all that stuff that I thought had happened had actually happened or was I just hallucinating. They said, "If you were hallucinating, we were all hallucinating." So I guess it either happened or it was a mass hallucination. Later, on another visit, I went to see the double doors that had been installed and learned that the people who had bought that house really liked them. That they appreciated them made me feel better.

Tennessee Again

When I got back to Tennessee, I went to Knoxville to see an Ibsen play being put on by my theater friends. After the play, I was up in the balcony with a friend looking down at another good friend who had been playing the lead. I gave her a pretty good mental twist and she spun around in a circle then looked up at us. We waved and smiled. Later, I and the friend who had been with me upstairs were outside lying in the grass.

"You have a lot of personal power," she said.

"Yeah," I said, "and I've found that if I wait long enough without doing anything at all, that power will get bored and, thank God, go away. And then I miss it terribly."

My parents had a candle shop in Gatlinburg. I had some of my sculpture tools there and also did pastel portraits. This was where I earned my money and, of course, I tried to use my "powers" to my advantage. Unfortunately it just didn't seem to work that way. I could 'push' someone at a garage sale or a flea market to give me a pretty low price sometimes. Like ask, "How much will you take for that," then mentally 'push' a soft mental "five dollars" when it was marked fifteen or twenty dollars. But they often do that when they're not pushed. Or I could, when I saw a police cruiser driving in front of me, 'push' a hungry stomach feeling and "Damn, that doughnut shop looks good." But they might have been ready to turn around anyway. Once I used the power to produce a quick pick lottery ticket for sixty-three dollars by feeling way out there in computer land and coming back to the machine that was picking it with near perfect timing. Six numbers would have been perfect. Oh, well, since none of that worked consistently for me, I earned my way by doing sculptures and pastel portraits.

Sculpture of Child

One rainy, stormy day early in the afternoon, a thunderstorm came through with lots of crashing thunder, and with the lightening popping and snicking around in the electric wiring. I had been working at my table doing some sculpting and got up to see how bad the storm was. A voice in my head said, "If you stand right there by that cabinet for the next thirty minutes, you won't be struck by lightening. But if you move from that spot you will be struck." So I stood there amid the crashing thunder and snicking lightening for about ten minutes and then said to myself, "Oh, crap. I'm not doing this." I walked over to the doorway leading to the creek and sure enough BLAM! I was hit with a jolt like from an electric fence. I thought "Well, that wasn't so bad." and went back to work.

As the line between my real world and my mental world became less clearly defined, most of my sculpting began to be done in both the real world and in the psychic world. I would imagine all sorts of things as I hammered the metal and welded it together.

While visiting the World's Fair in Knoxville, I had seen a wonderful hammered copper sculpture of a samurai warrior. It was sculpted in Russia and I had been impressed with the clothing that had sharply hammered edges. At about that same time I had read in a magazine that Tito, the president of Yugoslavia, had a workshop in the basement of his house where he did metal work, most of the time hammering on copper.

As I worked, I remembered this tidbit, and I imagined that a powerful man like that surely would have quite a psychic component to his work. Shortly afterward, as I was working on a sculpture of a goat at my table, I saw out of the corner of my third eye two glowing, St. Elmo's fire like arms approaching. Not realizing what was going on, I left my hand under the work too long, and as the arms came together, the pile of bricks were knocked out from under the goat and pinched the crap out of my finger. "That was the clincher!" growled a voice in my head. "You were lucky that time." I thought it was Tito responding to my invasion of his mind. Until then I had barely even thought about the offensive possibilities of psychic action.

When my children were small, I used them for models for full sized figures. People saw these displayed in my parents' candle shop and wanted some sculptures of their own children, so I began making full-sized hammered copper figures of children. Sometimes, I would imagine I was making a suit of armor that would protect the children from harm. One of these sculptures was of a little boy in Georgia. The night before I was to go to deliver the finished sculpture I went to a beer bar in town to relax. When I walked in I was mildly surprised to find Jason, our big black dog, sitting in a booth with a friend of mine drinking his beer out of a bowl on the table. I had heard that this was a fairly common occurrence there but had never seen it first hand. After we had had a few beers we were getting kind of tipsy. The general level of revelry and energy was rising along with the noise level in the bar.

My friend suddenly looked at me seriously and said, "My jaw just popped."

I looked back at him and shrugged and raised my eyebrows.

"In my family that means that one of my ancestors wants to communicate with me. It's a family thing, and when I'm under stress or when my ancestors want to communicate with me, my jaw pops."

I jokingly grabbed the web between my thumb and first finger and said, "I have an old war wound here and I get a little twinge of pain in it when my ancestors want to get my attention."

Immediately someone plunked some beers down on the table and yelled into the crowd, "I'm setting up this table! Here you go, boys."

"What's he mean by that?" I asked my friend.

"Don't know. Drink up," said my friend, raising his glass to toast the moment.

We clicked mugs and drank the beer.

Later that night after one of the more prominent local businessmen had arrived with his entourage and was enjoying the offerings of the beer bar, I was listening to the music and imagining the river flooding the town and removing the human induced infection from the natural beauty of the area. It seemed like everyone was getting higher and higher or at least drunk and drunker. The evening soon lifted off and I abandoned my attempt to manifest a flood and joined the party. Closing time came and went with little notice, His Prominence's presence granting a de facto variance in the liquor ordinance. Eventually I found my way through the toilet line to the urinal and began to pee. Much to the consternation of the sizable line of fidgeters behind me, I was still pissing a good stream about ten minutes later. I know I couldn't hold that much beer so where did it come from? Maybe it was some form of teleportation. I just don't know.

The next day I set off for Georgia to deliver the sculpture. On the way, there was a restaurant and gift shop with some bears outside in cages. During the course of doing the sculpture, I had passed these bears quite a few times, each time stopping to visit and had gotten to know the bears. There was a big burly male who paced back and forth like a fox in a cage, except instead of emanating fear and, "Please let me go." this one emanated anger, and "I'll eat your ass in a heartbeat if you give me a chance."

Another big one just lay around and didn't emanate anything. I think it was a big female. The third was just as sweet as she could be. About half the size of the other two and very playful, she would make eye contact easily and was just very nice. She was usually pretty friendly to me, I think she was getting to know me, but she seemed to be depressed that day. She looked sick, and there was some reddish diarrhea splashed around in the cage.

I went inside the restaurant and told the man behind the counter about the bear looking sick. He just said, in a mind your own business manner, no it wasn't sick and that it was all right.

I headed on down the road with the sculpture and soon stopped to pick up an old man who was hitchhiking. He had a mighty strong twinkle in his eye and I mentioned to him that a nice little bear was back there and how I thought it was feeling bad.

When he got out of the car just about three miles down the road, he said, "Bye. I'll see you soon."

I thought and said, "Well, probably not. Have a good time."

"Oh, Yeah, I'll be seeing you soon," he emphasized with his eyes twinkling.

I drove on down to Georgia and delivered the sculpture. While visiting with the couple getting the sculpture I felt a rapid increase in the density of the energy in the extra sensory world and then heard a wham as someone ran into a tree just in front of the house. We all went out to investigate. No one had been hurt but it was a scary time for all. Later that evening just before starting to eat an early dinner, the energy increased again and this time focused on the father's plate.

I muttered under my breath, "That's the clincher." The father picked up his practically uneaten plate of food and threw its contents into the trash.

"Aren't you going to eat anything?" His wife asked him.

"I don't feel hungry anymore," he snapped.

Bear Story

Shortly after dinner I started the trip back. Just before I got on the interstate I stopped at a convenient market to fill up with gas. The cashier was about my age and was missing his left arm from the elbow down.

"What happened?" I asked him, pointing to his arm.

"Just take your change and get the hell out of here, you hippie son of a bitch! It's none of your God damned business," he frothed. "We go to Vietnam to get the hell shot out of us for nothing, and then we get back and you accuse us of killing women and kids for fun! Get the fuck out of here!"

I left without a word. He was in worse shape than I was. On the interstate I was thinking about three or so fantasies at once: The bear was sick; my "old war wound;" the THEY who seemed to be handling me. Maybe I should just take the bear out of its cage and take it to a zoo or turn it loose in the national forest. Why did I say that I had an old war wound when I didn't? Sure it was in jest at the time. But people who really do have wounds have some reason to be sensitive about them.

My thoughts ran roughly like this as I drove. Who are THEY? I remember picking up a hitchhiker pretty close to home and letting him stay the night. He said THEY were after him and hounded him always. He thought they were in the sun among other places. Later on I too wondered if they were in the sun. How else could I explain the unwavering synchronicity of events? Of course THEY could be some sort of government agents. Perhaps there was a secret military program to investigate the possibility of psychic warfare. Maybe I was just crazy. I really think I should just get that bear out of that cage. I have a big can of corned beef. She would like that.

That time I ran out of gas. Just seconds later the guy on the motor cycle came asking to help. I say, "No one gets to go upstairs." Just minutes later in the middle of the night someone came wanting to go upstairs. Maybe that guy is so mad he just lost it and is coming after me. I really think I should get that bear out of there. Maybe someone is after me. She had red diarrhea. Is God trying to teach me something about not lying about war wounds? Are my ancestors trying to tell me something? Oh, I really have to stop to piss.

I turned onto a side road to look for a private place. About a mile up the road, after driving up a hill where I could look out over the city where the bear lived, I found a place to turn around and pull off the road. *I really should do something about that bear,* I was thinking. I got out of the car, stretched, and walked about twenty feet down the road and then turned toward the ditch. My feet hit something on the ground. I reached down and picked up a full beer bottle. Pissing into the grass, I thought, "Hmmm. It looks like a perfectly good bottle of beer. Maybe the police were following someone and after going around this curve he threw it out. Maybe some evil entity in my head has led me to it and it's drugged or poisoned. It looks pretty old but unopened. It is a cool evening." I drank the beer and it tasted good. My "war wound" was giving me a twinge of pain and I remembered the bar in Gatlinburg. Driving back down toward the main road, I still felt like someone was following me. It was about two in the morning and no one was in sight anywhere. I really should do something about that bear, I was thinking. Then I decided.

"OK, I'll get the bear out of the cage, but you have to give me clearance," I said to the voices in my head.

"What do you mean, 'Clearance'?" They answered.

"I mean no interference. Just me and the bear. Clearance." I emphasized.

After what seems like some consultation the voice said, "OK, you have the clearance."

"Are you absolutely sure?" I asked.

"Yes."

I pulled into the deserted parking lot and backed up to the door of the bear cage, opened the rear of the Pinto station wagon, and placed blankets over a fence and over a board that reached from the cage to the car. This made a lane that, hopefully, the bear would go down without becoming distracted. I opened the can of corned beef. Oh, it smelled good. Then I pried the lock off of the cage. Speaking in a very calm voice, I coaxed the bear out of the cage and almost to the car. A car pulled into the parking lot and stopped just short of my makeshift barrier.

"What the hell is this?" I asked the voices in my head, and then calmly to the bear "It's O K; let's just get on into the car."

A man got out of the car and leaned on the temporary railing, "Hey, Cindy! You won't believe this shit, man," he hollered. "He's got the bear out of the cage."

The bear was getting nervous. I spoke with a calm voice to the newcomers. "Just calm down and get back into your car. I'm moving the bear because she is sick."

"God damn, Cindy, get your ass out here. You got to see this," he hollered again, waving his beer.

The bear started moving back and forth faster, getting confused.

"Just relax and back away from the fence and for God's sake don't talk," in my most relaxing and calm voice.

The girl got out of the car and came to the fence. "Holy shit, Jake I thought you were joking," she hollered at Jake who was standing right next to her. "He's got the bear out a' the cage!"

The bear was getting more and more excited. She brushed the blanket one time too many, and it fell to the ground revealing her pile of dog food cans. It was her food stash.

I said in my calm voice, "Check out this yummy corned beef, huh, it's really good."

The girl hollered, "He's trying to feed her corned beef."

The bear turned, knocked the can away, and bit the crap out of my hand. "Oh, Shit!" I said, realizing I'd completely lost the situation.

Immediately the bear put her paws on the top of her head and cringed. "It's OK; I know you were just excited and confused. I said to her." She ran back into her cage.

Jake said to Cindy, "Let's get out of here before someone comes."

I threw the blankets into the car and drove off. My hand was screaming with pain. About a mile down the road I thought, *"Damn, I didn't lock the cage. What if she gets out and hurts someone?"*

A gas station was open at the intersection with the Interstate so I pulled in. With my hand wrapped in a bloody T shirt, I told the clerk, "I was trying to take the bear back there to get some help, but she bit me and I forgot to lock her cage back."

"Why'd ya do that?" he asked.

"Publicity stunt," I yelled as I ran out the door thinking to myself, "That ought to stop any publicity."

I pulled onto the interstate, visions of taking the bear to the woods or maybe to the zoo in Chattanooga vividly fading.

I screamed in my head, "You said I'd have clearance, you even checked to see if it was all right! What the hell happened?"

"We got worried about you. Sorry."

"Aw, shit! This hand hurts!"

I started wondering what might happen if the bear went back out of the cage in a confused psychotic state. My thoughts were, "She really is a nice bear, that won't happen. But what if it does? She bit the crap out of your hand you know. That was really that big bully of a shit bear though. Him pacing back and forth all day...I saw that energy fly to her just before she bit me. Yeah that and the clincher. Some old dude or doll with a paper puncher way, way in the background. But you don't know. You just don't know. What if someone was to get hurt? My hand was aching.

A few miles down the interstate I came up behind a state trooper's car. I flashed my lights at it until the driver waved me in front, and then I pulled over with the cruiser behind me. My hand was all bloody and wrapped in my T-shirt, so I held it behind me and walked toward the cruiser. Just as I reached the headlights, the trooper hollered for me to stop and put my hands up. I couldn't see him because the lights were still blinding me, but as I kept walking I pulled my hand from behind me and started to raise both of them. As I passed the lights I could see again, and the trooper started screaming at me to stop. I stopped about a foot away from his gun that pointed at my chest and said "Whoa!"

He told me to get back into the light in front of the car. I did, realizing I'd almost been shot. I told the troopers (there were two of them) about the bear, and that I was worried that I didn't lock the cage and that I needed to go to the hospital. So they arrested me. Here I just can't remember exactly what happened when. I think I followed them in my car to the police station in Chattanooga where they then arrested me and took me to the hospital. They most probably didn't want blood in their cruiser. I have visions of parking in the police chief's parking spot and telling them to not mess with my engine because it was special, and my putting a piece of tape on the hood so I could tell if anyone had opened it. But when I picked up my car, it was in the town where the bear lived. Anyway, they took me to the hospital in Chattanooga and guarded me so I wouldn't escape. After quite a wait, all the while in considerable pain, I went in to see a doctor. Or, rather,

94

the doctor came into the room to see me. He unwrapped my hand and gently washed it and probed the wound. He asked me what happened. I told him about the bear and that I really didn't think she meant to bite me. That it was the big bear in the cage coming through psychically and really that it probably was someone with a paper punch who actually did it. And then I described how she put her paws over her head right afterward to sort of apologize.

The doctor listened through all this as he was examining and cleaning, then as he pushed his hemostat through the hole in my hand, he said,

"You could have been shot." Then he looked questioningly at the trooper. The trooper looked kind of sick, realizing once again that he almost killed me.

"Yeah, I could have been," I replied.

"What do you do for a living?" he asked.

"I do sculptures mostly in copper and bronze." I said.

"An artist," he exclaimed. "That's good. Well, you will need this hand to work well for you so I'll do my best to fix it up."

I started to feel sorry for myself and sort of wanted to cry, and the doctor said, "That's sympathy. Hang on to that. It helps."

As he pushed first one, then another piece of plastic tubing through the hole he gave a running commentary, "This is a trick I learned in Vietnam. If you put just one drainage tube through the hole, the flesh seals around it and prevents it from draining. But if you put two side by side they will let the wound drain. Then to remove them you pull the ends of each of them on either side of the wound. That way when you pull them out, they don't pull germs through the wound. In about ten days you need to get these tubes out and maybe get some more antibiotics. Now, be sure to tell the doctor who takes these out that there are two of them in there, because it really looks like just one and they will clip one end off and accidentally leave the other one in there. Look at me, this is important. Be sure to tell the doctor who takes these tubes out that there are two of them."

I said, "OK."

While wrapping my hand in a thick layer of gauze he gave me instructions, "If you can hold your hand high it will hurt a lot less, and you should flex your fingers and thumb. Just get into the habit of holding your hand up and flexing the fingers and thumb so that it will heal without becoming stiff and an impediment to your artwork."

"Like this?" I held my hand up and flexed my fingers. "Ow."

"It will hurt for awhile," he said. Then, almost whispering, "I know that you can stand a lot of pain but a lot of people can't, so I'm giving you a prescription for pain medicine."

The policemen and I got the prescription filled and off we went back to the town where the bear cage was. It is also the County Seat. I was worried about not locking the cage back and had visions of the bear freaking out and killing someone and me spending the rest of my life in jail. The officers were real grim looking, and when I asked them about the bear they just grunted that they didn't know anything. After about a thirty or forty-five minutes ride, we got to the jail and I was processed, my pockets emptied, picture taken, finger printed except for some on my left hand. And the iron door slammed behind me.

"I told you I'd be seeing you again," said the now still tipsy old man with the twinkling eyes.

"I guess you were right after all. How did you know?" I asked.

He tapped his head saying "Some things you just know."

I still didn't know if the bear had hurt anyone and if I was going to stay behind bars forever. I sat on a lower bunk bed immersed in my totally miserable thoughts, staring at the wall on the other side of the room.

The wall was constructed of red primed steel held in place by 4" x 4" angle iron spaced about 4 feet apart. About 20 feet away from me, right in the middle of the wall, was one of the braces. If I were to run into that like I ran into the electric pole, it would surely kill me. And all this trouble would be over. Maybe. What if I were rushed to the hospital and survived as a near-basket case with a whole bunch more troubles than I have now? Sort of like what happened when I ran into the pole to commit suicide but much worse.

Instead I got up to use the nasty dirty stainless steel, stainless my ass, combination toilet sink and, still thinking I may be here a long time, said, "Good God, this place is a pig sty!" There was a can of cleanser sitting on a shelf with some paper towels. I scrubbed the sink/toilet contraption, read aloud the ingredients on the cleanser label, asked if there are any chemists in the place, and with visions of chemicals from different sinks and toilets in the building coursing through the pipes, I dumped a bunch more cleanser in the toilet and flushed. I counted aloud to three and said, "Flush." then, "Four." Pause. "And, flush" The chemicals in the vision mix in the pipes and "Kaboom!" My roommates looked at me like I was crazy.

I don't know if I'd gotten anything else across. I hoped they had watched MacGyver on TV. I lay down. I remembered the lottery ticket episode. So I went way out into the universe and came back as a contracting sphere sifting through pages of drawings and images of the inside of locks and their keys until I saw in my mind a brass key slipping into the cell lock and the door opening. With my eyes now open I heard the trustee calling my name. As I got up to go I saw the old man standing by the door ready to leave. The Trustee told him to go out to the office door, and took me to another cell, this one painted white. He told me that court is at nine and that I might want to clean up first, and motioned to the shower stall standing beside the fused sink toilet contraption. The occupants of this cell looked a little more permanent. In the corner farthest from the door resided a surly man with the company store, a half a bed full of stuff. The cement floor was crusted with God knows what.

I said to the Trustee, "I need a mop."

"Why?" he asked.

"Cause this place is disgusting." I pointed at the floor. "What is that stuff?"

"OK," he said.

The Trustee brought the mop and I mopped the floor, getting closer and closer to the guys in the corner "store". Every so often they looked over at me and scowled. They looked at each other and wondered what was about to happen as I got closer to them. When I got to their bunk I said, "Lift your feet." They did and I mopped under them. I put the mop in the bucket and leaned it on the wall by the cell door. As I started to strip to take my shower the Trustee came to take me to the courthouse. I told him just a minute, jumped in the shower and quick washed myself. I got out and there was no towel. I ran naked and wet to the "store," asked if I could borrow the towel, said "thanks," without waiting for a reply, dried and dressed, took the towel back and said "Thanks again," and swooped out with the Trustee.

At some time I must have called home because there in the courtroom sat my mother and brother. I guessed they'd been busy since they got my call. It was about a three-hour drive from home. I stood up before the Judge and he told me how bad I'd been. (I could tell he was a bit amused). He read from a paper then told me that if I would plead guilty to shoplifting a bear from a gift shop and pay $75 restitution and court costs, he would let me go. I asked him if that was a felony, he said no, and so I said yes. I went back to the jail to get the contents of my pockets.

I asked, "Where are my pills?"

"What pills?" he said, looking at the ceiling.

"My pain pills?" I asked.

"They aren't on the list," he said.

We went to retrieve my car. I checked the hood and saw that it'd been opened, paid the money and headed home.

My mother said, "A man from a radio station called and left his number, do you want to call him?"

"No," I said.

"Well, why not."

"Because I told some guys at a gas station that I did it as a publicity stunt," I told her.

"Why'd you do that?" she said, rubbing her forehead.

"Because it wasn't," I said.

"Well, why don't you call him just to see what he does?" she asked.

We stopped near the town the radio station was in and called. The radio personality said he no longer wanted to speak to me.

My mother said, "That was quite a finesse you pulled off."

I still don't quite know what she meant by that. When I got back home the focus was on my hand. Since I was such a "talented artist," the opinion was that I should get the most talented hand treatment available. This required a trip to Kentucky, as our "circle" had concluded that the best hand doctor worked near a hospital up there. After faithfully making everyone think I was waving to them because I held my big white hand high and flexed my fingers for a week or so, I went to see the hand doctor. As he came into the room he seemed busy, talking with another doctor and waving a sheaf of papers.

He sat down, unwrapped my hand and said, "This seems to be healing well. Let's just take this tube out and give you some more antibiotics."

I said, "There are two tubes there."

"Yes, we will just pull it out and everything seems to be healing just fine." He was ignoring what I'd said. As he sniped off one end of the tube and pulled the other end, he said, "There, now just bandage it back up, would you Martha?"

I quickly thought *it might be cool to have a pierced hand, but it might get infected. No. Maybe I could sue the doctor for malpractice, but my hand might get screwed up in the process. Again, no.*

As he turned to leave I grabbed his arm and looked him in the eye saying, "There were two tubes in there so the wound could get better drainage. You just snipped the end off of one and pulled the other one out, leaving the snipped one in there."

He sat back down waving the nurse out of the way, found the end of the one he had snipped off and pulled it out, then looked at me meaningfully and whispered, "Thank you."

Weather and Visits from the Dead

I tried my damnedest to talk the weather into washing Gatlinburg away but never got it to cooperate. Sometimes when there were thunderstorms coming through, I imagined that I could see and feel the entire frontal system and feel the energy riding up and down the front on long strings of lightening. My house was pretty airy in the winter so I was very interested in the weather.

If a cold front was approaching, I would try to imagine any number of scenarios to make it come in a warmer state. Once I tried to get it to dive underground as our reality went above it. That time it seemed to actually work. Sometimes I was interested in swapping our weather fronts with warmer climes. I even called the NSA once to see if they could arrange a swap with South America because it was getting so hot down there. The young man on the phone was very polite, but I could tell he thought I was crazy.

About a week later the Falklands war broke out. But they still didn't send us any heat. Another time when there was going to be a real hard freeze I said to myself, "Oh, Crap." and just reached out in frustration to all the atoms in the valley and gave them a terrific jerk as if I was starting a chain saw. Instead of the hard freeze we got a temperature of about 45 degrees. The weather forecasters said that a freak wind had come over the mountain and compressed the air so it warmed up. Whatever.

I had been dating a particularly nice young woman for some time and so it was natural for that marriage ditty to keep running through my mind. Something old, something new.... The two of us were cleaning and preparing an old cabin my family owned and these old, new, borrowed, blue things were popping up. It seemed to me that in this process another couple began to inhabit our bodies along with the two of us. They were from some years ago and often smiled fondly at each other.

101

One day, still out at the old cabin and in this happy frame of mind, I for no apparent reason felt like walking up into the woods towards the top of the low ridge behind the cabin. There I discovered a cleanly cut vertical hole about two feet deep and about six inches in diameter. Such a hole as could have been dug with a posthole digger except there was no indication of any disturbance in the leaves and pine needles around the hole. No dirt pile. A twig and a small leaf in the bottom indicated to me that it hadn't been there very long. I asked a friend what he thought about finding the hole and he surmised that I had followed a trail of psychic energy left by another up to the hole.

My father had told me of some holes that fit that description. They had been discovered on a ridge a few miles away after a particularly fierce thunderstorm. I never saw them but they sounded very similarly mysterious. As to what the hole was or why it was there? We just didn't know any more than my father and his friends had learned about the holes they had discovered. Nothing.

During that relationship I had been collecting the old and the new things as I came across them at my house. I had an old rust-pitted double-bit ax head that I had dug up while leveling the floor of the barn that I was remodeling into a house. This I placed next to the newer one that our family had used when we built our cabin in northern Wisconsin. Digging farther I discovered an old shovel rusted and with no handle. Seeing it next to the new one I was digging with so soon after pairing the axe heads, reinforced the idea of collecting these old and new things with my girlfriend.

One morning shortly thereafter I was dreaming that my Grandma, my Uncle and his daughter (all deceased) came to visit me. They walked up the driveway to my house and I could see them through the wall of the house as their bodies were glowing and they also had very bright auras. When they got to the door there was a knock on my real door and I woke up to answer it. The man I had bought the farm from was standing there with his wife and daughter. I tried to talk to them from two points of view simultaneously, both as if they were my relatives and also as if they were my neighbors.

"Hi, I haven't seen you all in a long time. And who is this? (Safely indicating both daughters whom I'd never met, since my cousin died before I was born).

"This is my daughter. You haven't met her before. We were just passing by after church and thought we would see how you were doing."

"Well, it certainly is a surprise to see you all this morning. It sure looks like it's going to be a bright day today. You three look like you are just glowing with health," I said, talking to all of them.

"Yes, it feels good just to be alive today."

Then they asked if I had a washing machine hose and I found an old one but it wasn't the type they were looking for. Soon we all said our good-byes and my neighbors walked away down the hollow and my relatives parted from them, still glowing and walked into the hillside by the house. By then I was pretty wide-awake, but I fixed some coffee anyway.

Bugs and Orion

Orion:

> *A giant hunter noted for his beauty. He was blinded by Enopian, but Vulcan sent Cedalion to be his guide, and his sight was restored by exposing his eyeballs to the sun. Being slain by Diana, he was made one of the constellations and is supposed to be attended by stormy weather.*
> > *Brewer's Dictionary of Phrase and Fable*

The constellation Orion is pictured as a giant hunter with belt and sword surrounded by his two dogs and other animals....

I had been watching TV pretty consistently and had begun to feel as though an entity was able to communicate with me telepathically using that medium. It seemed that there was an entity wanting to settle down in the hollow, and it wanted assurances that it would be all right to do that. I allowed that it would be not only be OK to have such a neighbor but would probably be pretty interesting and exciting. This entity seemed to be operating in the worlds I mentioned earlier that are composed of the "Magic of the Senses" and telepathy. Worlds where a virtual "body" could be formed by using telepathic links and bits and pieces of existing matter, live and "dead". I was watching an afternoon talk show with three women discussing something when the telepathic link began working. A parallel thought thread came through from one of the theater group's plays where a disembodied voice from above had dictated or suggested artistically the actions of the actors. It seemed to me that the women on the TV were for their first time trying out a little radio hearing aid device that was used as a prompter. I remember one of them saying "Wow! That sure is different," and I wondered if she was referring to the telepathic connection or to the little ear devices. Or, was she possibly referring to something else entirely?

I could still see into the hillside in the direction my relatives had gone, and I was marveling more and more as the mysteries of the day unraveled. As I passed some boxes of books upstairs a voice in my head said, "You'll find it in the bottom of that box." I stopped and looked through the box and on the bottom was a small book of poetry with pictures added by a child. The book had been given to my Uncle by my Grandmother and had crayon pictures drawn in it by his daughter. I looked at the book, "reading" it, and could feel their spirits again. I marveled anew at the day's progress.

Then I noticed an old and rusting can of foam carpet cleaner in an adjacent box and started to take it down the stairs to put it next to the new can I had recently bought. The one I hadn't been able to use, because I didn't have a vacuum cleaner. On the way down the stairs the can took on a life of its own and it leaped up out of my hands. As I bobbled it, the rascal flipped upside down and squirted a blob of carpet cleaner into the palm of my hand. The stairway from the upstairs led straight to the open door of the house. I set the can down and headed out the door to the creek to rinse my hands.

As I approached the creek I was surrounded by blue energy which grew in intensity as I neared the creek. When I reached down towards the water, the energy concentrated and surged through me. For a moment my body turned a transparent blue, and as the energy passed, it picked up a black lump in my chest that I had thought might be cancer. As the lump sped down through my arms and hands towards the water it broke into smaller pieces and, with audible popping noises, bugs of different types materialized from the black spots and fell into the creek. The blue energy kept going through the ground and into the hillside my relatives had walked into. I immediately dropped to my knees and examined the approximately three dozen bugs as they scampered away on the bottom of the creek. Some of them seemed to look like little rocks with legs (I never confirmed this and wonder if I was mistaken about these). Some looked like those rolly polies you find under rocks but more flat and more accustomed to the water, sort of like small trilobites. And some were bugs that looked like they would grow wings. I caught one of the latter and looked at it for a long time. I hoped I didn't hurt it when I caught it because I was thinking that this was a collection of bugs and whatnot that was making up the "magic of the senses"/telepathic virtual reality. And that this bug might have been part of the "entity" that had been negotiating with me to live here.

I didn't know exactly what had happened. The bug I had looked at for the longest time wasn't one I had ever noticed seeing before. Neither were the trilobite shaped ones. So I locked the house and started to walk to U. T. in Knoxville with my two dogs. I figured this would give me time to think about what had happened, and that the library at U.T. would be open by the time I got there. I soon met some of my neighbors who were putting up a fence by the road and I told them that something weird had happened up in my hollow and that they shouldn't go up there until I got back. Shortly after that another neighbor came by in his pickup truck and gave me and the two dogs a ride out to the highway where he let us out, because he was going the other way.

Our walk was pretty uneventful at first. The sun set and the night fell around us as I tried to grasp what had happened. Trilobites to me are symbolic of time travel, fossils that they are, and I had made a sculpture of a bowl of trilobites with a spoon sticking out called "Trilobite Soup." Was there a time travel component to this? They did look sort of like trilobites. Like flat rolly polies or segmented roaches. The bugs with the trident tails might refer all the way back to those tri-recorder things in the sky. Pebbles with legs, I decided, were my imagination. Magic of the senses type composite creatures could now be living in the hollow. There was the appearance or feeling of some sort of agreement being presented and that golden helix DNA halo/mind clamp. My long dead relatives seemed to have something to do with what happened. Maybe people do live on after death. Maybe some areas need to be set aside for different realities to coexist. All this excitement and talk had tired me out

I lay down to rest beside the road, Jason the dog lay next to me and the dog Lincoln continued his orbit at about 100 feet. I was facing south and there was Orion in the clear twinkling sky. As I watched, Orion glowed brighter and began to move, the picture of the constellation walked across the sky using whatever stars were available to anchor his knees, hands, head, belt and shield. As he passed, the stars first brightened and then dimmed. He quickly reached the horizon and for a moment I thought he was gone. Then, as all around me became excited with energy and my body became covered with goose bumps, Orion's body entered mine from beneath the ground and stood me up in one smooth motion.

Energy was everywhere almost crackling with anticipation as he spoke into my head, "Well, do you know how to build a fire?"

"I guess I do, didn't Prometheus teach us that?" I nodded my head toward the streetlights and the light streaming from the homes and businesses in the distance.

"No, I mean a 'FIRE'," he said as he grabbed me by the heartstrings.

"Whew." I said, "Yeah, I guess I do," as I felt thoughts fly, contra thoughts fly, and emotions blazed in the distance as couples burst into heated arguments for no reason.

We began to walk. Jason orbited at about thirty feet, guarding me. Lincoln orbited at about one hundred yards, scouting everything out and coming back occasionally to report, and to check that Jason and I were still okay. A little ways down the hill there was evidence of a long ago wreck. The passage through the trees was marked with twisted re-growth of the smaller trees and scarred areas of missing bark on the larger ones. With my "Orion" senses I could see that deep at the end of the lane of crushed and broken trees a "spirit" was laying there reliving the wreck and still stuck there after many years. Orion mentally attached a neon red colored cable of light to the "spirit" and hooked it to the next passing car. The light stretched taut and down the road went the "spirit", off to join in the wonders of the afterlife. The trees were finally freed of their psychic mold of horror and could begin to heal their wounds.

We continued towards Knoxville, stopping occasionally to pull out more stuck spirits. I wondered if anyone was home at a friend's house and sat beside the road. I thought I should be able to tell and yet I couldn't. I remembered the last time I was there her father had been angrily mowing the grass as he flung his push-type rotary mower at the grass with a passion. I had almost stopped him because I had seemed to see his daughter there in the grass. I had asked him where she was and he had stopped long enough to tell me he had just the day before told her he wasn't going to support her any more. He kind of reminded me of another friend who would chop wood by imagining the head of someone he didn't like sitting on the chopping block and then splitting it in two. Come to think of it, his wife kept getting migraines. Anyway, I didn't even know whether or not she still lived there so I continued on my way.

Most of the time while walking that night I felt like I was up in the stars with the image of my "reality" superimposed as a three-dimensional overlay on the cosmos. Maybe because that's the way Orion lived. Later Orion and I were walking along in this 3-D cosmic overlay and I was thinking of this girl I know. My foot slipped off the edge of the pavement and as I was kind of twisting my ankle a little while trying to recover my balance, I noticed the girl was very small and slipping down the edge of the pavement but was still inside my foot so I said, "Oops, sorry." She seemed to be OK, So I carried on.

I began to get hungry and to think about food and different diets and their moral advantages and shortcomings. Immediately, wild onions popped up along the road. By popping up I mean that they seemed to grow up before my eyes, not that I was just noticing them. I wasn't hungry enough to eat them though. Orion said I didn't need any food like that, I could just eat energy, and then told me that, by the way, eating just energy was just as morally reprehensible as cannibalism because that's all we are anyway. I still didn't want to eat the onions. It was neat how they seemed to appear just when I thought of food. I probably smelled them. It seems real odd but I did see them growing up.

Orion asked me, "Do you want to see me stop the next car?"

I said, "Sure."

Lincoln stopped his orbiting and ran down the far side of the road and at the same time Jason ran down the road on this side. They stopped opposite each other about one hundred yards down the road and looked across at each other. A red beam of light stretched across the road between their eyes. A car came over the small hill and just before reaching the red beam of light, stopped, backed up, and pulled into the driveway of a house that I learned months later was a veterinarian's office.

The dogs blinked and the beam shut off and we all went on down the road. Orion knew I was impressed and unable even to begin to imagine explaining how that had happened. I told him, "I'd have been impressed if you'd just predicted that the next car was going to turn up the driveway."

Just as there are spots along a road where something terrible has happened, there also are spots that provide peace and recuperation. We would all lie down and rest whenever we reached one of these spots and I really appreciated them. Thirty years later as I drive the road I still see some of these spots that provided such good rest to us. Perhaps there is an emanation given off by places that remain unchanged for years. Whatever happens, they just glow with peace.

One of these places was the front yard of the place that once housed a visiting guru who I went to see. It was just before daylight and we all rested on the lawn. At first I worried that the present occupants of the house would be upset to find a man and his two dogs lying in their front yard, but no one seemed to mind, and the rest felt good and the peace was restorative. When daylight arrived we stopped at a Krystal to get hamburgers for all of us. We were all hungry in spite of all the energy we had been soaking up and we did get onions on the breakfast burgers they made for us.

When we got to the bridge over the Tennessee River we had walked about 21 miles and our feet were getting sore. Some good friends of mine lived on the other side of the bridge. We stopped there and after a brief explanation of our circumstances and a short nap, I left the dogs with them and went on to the University library to look up the bugs. At the library, I couldn't find pictures matching the rolly-polly / trilobites I had seen, and had pretty much decided that the rocks with legs had been just my imagination stretching the moment. I had gotten a real good look at one of the bugs in the creek after I had caught it and put it on a rock. While it clung to the rock underwater it seemed to communicate with me by hypnotically waving the little 'hairs' on it's back in synchronization with telepathy to assure me that everything would be all right. This one, with the triple tail and the segmented rear end and six legs and wavy things and antennae, was pretty easy to find in the research books. It was a Mayfly nymph, though it seems like it should have been a September or October fly nymph. It was a relief to find at least one of the kinds of bugs because it meant to me that I hadn't just hallucinated them. I still didn't know just what to do about all this so I asked a librarian who I might see about insects and their larvae. She referred me to the office of a bug specialist to ask him if he knew. Unfortunately his office was closed.

A couple of blocks away a good friend of mine had a metal sculpting studio so I went to see him. Outside of his studio was a fire truck and I was introduced to a fireman of some high rank. Orion's energy and spirit was still crackling around and I wondered if this fireman was connected to Orion's question about knowing how to start a fire, but I didn't want to open that Pandora's Box of insanity so I kept my mouth shut. I did ask what the fireman was doing in his store and was told that he just visited every so often because they were friends. Yeah, and he drives around town in his City fire truck just to visit his friends. It seemed as if there were knowing looks being shared, so I felt it was a bad time to ask my friend what he thought about the bugs. They did ask what I was doing and I told them I was just walking around.

I decided I could talk to my two girl friends who were camping by the lake. It was on the bus route, which I could catch about four blocks away over an old patched brick street which had somehow survived the centuries. So, I was walking along a small part of the old road from Washington D. C. to New Orleans. These old oaks and bricks had heard the horses and buggies and stagecoaches rattle and clatter by. They were still there looking and I wondered if they could see into the future. If they could see it, they didn't share it with me.

I sat on a bench at a bus stop and waited. I'd never ridden the Knoxville buses before but they were going my

111

way today. While I was waiting, a friend pulled to the curb in his metallic green dune buggy and asked me what I was doing there. I told him I was going out to the lake to see the girls and he offered to take me there. He put his beer on the dashboard and drove while holding an oil can out over the side of the car. He thought the oil can was leaking but I didn't see that. After a few stops we got to the lake. I found the girls and finally got around to asking them what they thought I might do about my bug problem. They didn't know what to do either, but the one who had been in my ankle told me she had fallen down a thirty-foot high cliff the night before and didn't even get a scratch. As it was getting dark, my friend with the dune buggy offered to take me back to town. On the way back we stopped to piss at an abandoned church and with my Orion senses working again, I stood there watching the spirits come and go from the graveyard, zipping up and into the sky and back. It looked like they were having fun.

I still didn't know if I should get together a team of experts to examine the creek but after I picked up the dogs and headed for home it started raining like hell and by the time we got home the creek was flooding. I just went to sleep.

Thunderstorm

There were thunderstorms, huge, powerful sentient beings strung into lines communicating in bolts of clarity carrying energy from Texas to Ohio or Canada. I had felt them coming closer and closer, until finally I saw one of them coming over the ridge. It spoke to me in its way, saying, "Let's go. Now!" In a flash of understanding I knew it was asking me to participate in a journey to the desert. A journey that would be sometimes up in the sky in full glory, and sometimes would remain beneath the consciousness, hidden from view in the secret places where thunderstorms go. I was at my parent's shop and told my mother, "I'm going to ride a thunderstorm to Arizona, and I have to leave now!" She nodded calmly, as if I'd said I was going to get some groceries.

I got in my car, let my dog Lincoln jump in as Jason stayed by my mother's side, and started for the interstate. The radio was on and the air was electrified and smelling of ozone and wet things. The storm's "entourage" was traveling with me. Just past Knoxville there was a tremendous blow in the psychic world. It felt like a semi trailer truck had t-boned us. I slowed down to consider this new development and the 'entourage' faltered and began to regroup. I sat just off the interstate, telepathically checking, as best I could, the wholeness of those near and dear to me. Everyone seemed to be feeling OK so I drove down to the next road. As I was wondering if this psychic blow was an omen sent to tell me not to take this trip, a song on the radio ended and the announcer came on. He said that after checking with the City Police, the County Sheriff's office and the Highway Patrol, he has found that no accidents have been reported within the last hour and that everything seems to be fine. Hmmm. So, I gathered myself together nodded to my dog and off we went again.

Driving down the road was wonderful. I must have

stopped somewhere to sleep because I remember being surprised to see that it was daylight again, but I didn't remember having stopped. Surely I hadn't driven for hours through the night in my sleep! My dog, Lincoln, was looking anxious, so we stopped in a grove of trees to give him a break and for me to nap.

When I woke up Lincoln was gone. I whistled and he didn't come running, so I whistled again, casting the sound through some mirror like puddles to the 'other side'. This time he came running and I fed him and told him how good he was. Because I still thought sometimes that I was being handled, it occurred to me to cover my car with a thin coat of mud to change the color, but I got into it without doing that and drove onto the interstate again.

The sun was shining and I was feeling fine. As I drove along the interstate I used the fingers of my phantom arm to gently flush the birds out of the forests, sending them flying across the road in front of me. People in other cars smiled and laughed and waved when I tapped their cars with joy as I passed them. I felt good.

Later, while driving through Memphis a beautiful woman with black hair and big brown eyes looked at me with a soulful come-hither look as I passed her car, staring soul to soul. I really wanted to stop to spend some time with her. I wondered how she could drive without looking ahead. In my rear view mirror I saw her car and another pull to the shoulder of the road. She was real good at her job.

At sunset I crossed the Mississippi river into Arkansas. I felt that the storm's energy was close, just the other side of the veil. I remember noticing after dark that I felt like I was flying again, literally flying an airplane. The fingernails of my little fingers were still painted red on the left and green on the right so I could familiarize myself with the orientation of the lights of my plane. I passed a hitchhiker dressed in a too-large white shirt and black pants. I would have picked him up but traffic was right behind me and the side of the road was narrow, so I passed him with a shrug.

About a half-mile up the road I saw him again, standing there in his loose white shirt and black pants and holding a small overnight bag. This time I did stop and as he got into the car I asked him if that had been him standing back there or did he have a twin traveling with him? I guess he didn't understand what I was talking about because he answered with something that I didn't understand. He didn't speak very good English. I got the impression he wanted to go to Little Rock where he had a home or knew someone who did, and I began to wonder if he was some sort of alien.

Since it was so hard to talk we settled in for the drive. I imagined the car lifting, the wheels retracting, my fingernails lit and the strobe light blinking into the night. The idea of his being an alien, as in from another planet, stuck in my mind, and I remembered a book about the hollow earth theory. The book described a hollow earth with another sun inside it and holes at the north and south poles that are always covered with clouds so they have escaped detection so far. The UFOs come and go through these holes. And it mentioned Admiral Byrd's report of flying over islands with palm trees as some sort of confirmation of the theory. Others have attributed Byrd's outlandish reports to carbon monoxide poisoning. In any case, it soon seemed that Admiral Byrd's spirit had come into my body and we were flying over ice and clouds and then looking down at islands with palm trees. We were of course still driving on the 'real' road. I gave the hitchhiker a sort of arched eyebrow look. He pointed at the floor through which the islands were visible and said in some language," Whew, that's pretty vivid."

After a while I realized we'd missed the turn into Little Rock. After looking at the map I discovered there was a road ahead which went through a park and over a ridge or a small mountain to the road we should have taken. At the entrance to the park there was a closed gate. While we were looking at the map again to see the shortest way to get back on track, a park ranger came down the road and let himself through the gate. We jumped out of the car and asked him if that road went into Little Rock and he said that it did, but it was closed for the night.

I said "But you have the key. You could let us go through."

He said, "Sure I could but I'm going home."

Pushing, I said that it was really important because I had picked up this hitchhiker and he needed to get to Little Rock. And that I really needed to get further west because if I didn't, the thunderstorm I'd been traveling with would leave me behind and if that happened I wouldn't be able to stay with the flow and I really needed to because it was building up again. He still didn't open the gate. While we were pleading with him, Lincoln was running into and out of the woods. Pushing again, I talked about what a nice view there must be from the top of the mountain. I could 'see' it in his head, so I amplified it. When it was positively glowing the city lay out below with the lights twinkling. I pushed harder, asking if he couldn't just drive over to take the hitchhiker across. He said he had to go home to his wife and kids.

Pushing, "It's OK" we said, "It's very late. They're asleep anyway."

Finally he looked at the sky and screamed, "I DON'T KNOW, I'M SO FUCKED UP NOW I CAN'T EVEN THINK. I'M GOING HOME!" And he got into his car and left us.

So we went back the way we had come, this time making our wrong turn right, and after dropping the hitchhiker off in Little Rock, I headed for Eureka Springs.

Later on I was hungry so I stopped at a small restaurant that looked like it served the home-cooked

116

meals I like. I pulled into the parking lot and went inside and sat down at a table. I sat and sat, looking around, but no one saw me. No one even looked at me. The plump middle-aged lady at the cash register didn't see me. The doe-eyed waitress so admired by her customers didn't see me. The other customers didn't seem to see me either. So I left still hungry, deciding that I must just be a ghost there. Maybe they just didn't like the looks of me and communally decided to ignore me. Maybe they were all ghosts and the place wasn't even open or there. I saw a Mexican restaurant and went in and was happy that everyone saw me and the waitress brought me plenty of food. There was a party of about ten at a table across the room all talking Spanish. I watched the thought forms coming and going around the table and seemed to be able to understand what was being said by watching the pictures. Everyone was very friendly and seemed happy, including me.

I got back on the road again but now I was getting sleepy. I stopped at a small motel to ask the rates and to get a pack of cigarettes. I couldn't afford the rates and they didn't take dogs, but when I paid for the cigarettes the lady behind the night window told me she thought I really should go to the hospital and gave me directions to it. When I got back in the car, I looked at myself in the rear view mirror and was relieved to see nothing alarming. No blood. No gore. I thought maybe she was psychic or something and seeing into the future so I stopped beside the road where the shoulder was real wide and after watering the dog and myself I climbed into the back and went to sleep.

I was flying surrounded by a bright white light when I was flung into my body by an even brighter bolt of lightening and an explosion of thunder. I awoke as the flash was scurrying across the landscape chased by its thunder. It was raining but the storm had mostly passed on. I figured this was a personal wake up call, so we got on the road again, stopping in a few miles at a bridge over a small river to take a bath and change clothes. I fed Lincoln and while he was eating I noticed a small orange cooler floating by. For some reason this convinced me that orange was the color of the day. When we got back into the car, I put an orange on the dashboard and up the road we went

Eureka Springs is in a valley and I was approaching on the road above the valley. I stopped at a small general store for gas and some snacks. The store was very busy and first I paid for my gas so I could get out of the way of the gas pumps, then got some snacks for breakfast. As an after-thought, I paid for some fruit. I kept thinking about transactional analysis and trying to keep the 'spaceship' properly balanced during this trading and transactional phase. After the rush of customers subsided, I took a friend's phone number from my wallet. He lived in town. I tried the pay phone. It didn't work.

Once again I approached the cashier, this time to ask for more change and where I might find a phone that would work. He said that a thunderstorm had passed through that morning and that it had probably hit the phone line tripping some breakers and that I could try the phone about a half-mile up the road because he thought it was on a different circuit. He also commented that he had had more transactions with me than with anyone else that morning. He seemed to be pleased by that notion. I felt pleased about it, too.

When I reached the phone booth the cashier had mentioned, I could see just a bit further down the road to the turn into the city, so I went to the turn only to discover a police car had blocked the road and was turning people back. There had been a wreck or a tree had blown down or Jesus fell over or something. I went back to try the phone. I tried about three times. Sometimes it would seem to be ringing but then the line would go dead. I was about to give it up and try the road again. By then I was thinking there was some plot to keep me from getting into town. I was beginning to suspect everyone of being party to it. But as I left the phone both another car pulled into the parking lot. A very nice looking young lady got out and asked me if the phone was working. I told her no, it wasn't. She suggested that maybe it would work if we both tried it. We both squeezed into the booth and put our quarters into the phone and it worked first for her then for me. We thanked each other and went our separate ways.

The spell or whatever was broken, and now there was no more trouble getting into town. I had directions to the house of another friend who lived there. Over coffee she told me that my other friend lived up on the lip of the valley. As it happens, I had driven by his house about six times while trying to get into the valley.

So I finally got to my friend's house on the lip of the valley and visited with him and his wife for awhile. In the evening as we sat on the porch, a thunderstorm danced in the valley before us. It seemed to approve of my taking a rest-stop along with the storm front. It also taught me something more about the language of storms.

On the far side of the road that ran in front of the house was a line of maple trees which in the dim light looked like snuggling heads of people. In the distance across the valley was a tree-covered ridge. Clouds were filling the valley and the thunderstorm advanced over the ridge line with the lightening flashing continuously. While I was imagining that a spiritual energy in the form of lightening was being exchanged from the storm to the earth and back to the storm, the clouds cleared for a few moments, revealing a huge sphere covered with smooth clouds and emitting bolts of lightening. It was slowly making its way westward. This was the face of the storm front that had called me out for this journey. Was its demand friendly or malevolent, I wondered?

The next morning I too went westward. In Oklahoma, just past Fort Pierce, I picked up another hitchhiker, a middle-aged Native American man. After riding for awhile he asked me if I would take him to the town he lived in, not far off the interstate, or so he said. Of course I agreed. I soon found out that "not far" was forty miles north. On the way up to the town we passed a Pentecostal Church and I asked the hitchhiker if that was the church that used peyote as a sacrament in its services. He said that he didn't go there and wasn't sure if they did or not. Then I asked him if he could get me some wine, in quarts, not fifths. He said that he might be able to arrange that. Near the center of the town the hitchhiker asked me to stop next to a small house. He jumped out of the car and was greeted by a small throng of people of all ages, his family, I found out later. Lincoln was super anxious to get out of the car and I warned him that he was very outnumbered by the dog pack surrounding the car and that he should behave himself if he wanted to stay alive. The small throng of people watched, a little tensed, as Lincoln jumped out of the car. Amazingly he did behave...just the usual standing stiff and sniffing and tail wagging. Everyone was relieved.

When I reminded my former rider about the quarts of wine, he went off to talk to some people and returned saying that I would have to be checked out by someone apparently named The German Woman. So off we went. It turned out that she lived in an old saloon. Since we were now on an Indian Reservation it was no longer used as a saloon but mostly as a sparsely stocked drug store with living quarters in the back. The German Woman came out of the living quarter area of the store. She was 'nize und t'ick' and dressed in a gray chintz dress that was a little too gray. The tiny pink flowers in the dress fabric had turned gray too. After looking at me for a few moments, she nodded approval to my Indian guide, and off we went to the barbershop. It was not far from the saloon, but we drove anyway, then climbed the ten or twelve steps to the door and knocked. The barber came to the door, looked up and down the street from his small elevated porch, and then let us in. There were three other people in the shop, including someone lying on the couch that looked quite dead. One of the men was leaving. The rest of us spent some time talking about the weather, the town, the politics of the nation, outer space and some local gossip for awhile, all done apparently in order to avoid going directly to the real reason I was there. But then I noticed that the man on the couch was slowly turning less and less gray and more and more pink and realized that this 'idle' prattle had been for his benefit. At last he gasped a breath, spluttered, coughed and struggled to a sitting position. I looked at the barber with a questioning look and he said, "Oh, we do it all the time here." I guess I had been cleared to receive because the man who had gone somewhere came back from there with my two quarts of wine. I thanked everyone all around, got Lincoln back into the car and though all of them asked me to stay longer and to have dinner with them and to party down with them, I politely refused. This "not far" journey had already taken me about eight hours so I felt kind of in a hurry. Simultaneously, I was feeling like just staying for dinner and partying and maybe settling down here for the rest of my life.

This urge was becoming stronger and stronger and was so scary that I decided I needed to reach some kind of escape velocity in order to break free. I put the accelerator to the floorboard heading west, and with the windows rolled down, began to scream. I screamed about how much I hated Indians and packs of flea-bitten dogs and T'ick German Women and barbers and especially screamed about how much I hated little-in-the-middle-of-flat-nowhere. All the time I was screaming, I felt that the Indians in the town who heard me understood exactly what I was doing and just regarded it as no more or less than a car leaving town with a loud muffler.

About ten miles out of town, I calmed down and

parked in a roadside picnic area to look at the map to see where I was headed. After feeding Lincoln, eating a snack and drinking a schloggle of wine, and listening to the prattle of migrating blackbirds, everything seemed OK again. I was headed west on a red highway beside a railroad track. There was a thunderstorm in the distance and except for a nearly empty gas tank all was well in my world. About ten miles farther at the next intersection there was a gas station all lit up and I drove right up to the pumps, right across some curbs by the road that I didn't see. I was afraid my tires had burst but decided that I should act like all was well, perfectly normal, so I got my gas and pulled back onto the road without looking at them. All was fine.

The next day I was supposed to meet my girlfriend at a lake that turned out to be run by the U. S. Army Corp. of Engineers. The place had a definite military aura about it, which made me uneasy. And it was big. After driving around the place for some time without seeing her, I finally chose a hilltop in a central location and began to wait. Lincoln was out scouting in ever-widening circles as I was impatiently pacing in ever smaller ones. I worried that I had somehow gotten into the wrong universe and twice retrieved Lincoln and drove around searching again. At last I got enough nerve to go ask at the gate and before I got to it, there she came. I was very relieved. After a nice picnic and some warm greeting we started off. We had two cars of course so we couldn't talk much, but our relationship contained a lot of silence anyway so that was kind of normal. It felt good to just be that close to her. By the time it got dark, we were in an Indian reservation. After getting some gas and using the rest room which was decorated with about four or five live scorpions crawling around on the wall in front of me as I pissed, I paid for the gas without using the hated Jacksons.

A few miles down the road we came to some roadside tables where we ate some supper cooked on a tiny Coleman stove, fixed our bedding in the car and went to sleep. A couple of hours later we were awakened by a pickup truck full of Indians pulling up and demanding that we get out of the car. I left a growling Lincoln in the car, sure that my girlfriend would let him out if it got ugly, and got out to ask what the matter was. They told me that since this was an Indian reservation and we weren't Indians we would have to leave right now. I said that we were really tired and had been driving all day and we really needed to stay the night to rest up for our trip tomorrow. They asked if I had ever heard of the Scorpions and I said yes, I had just seen four or five of them back there on the rest room wall. They asked if I had hurt them. I said no, that they weren't bothering me at all.

They looked at each other and said, "Well, you can stay the night if you give us ten dollars each."

I said "Oh, no! I don't have that much money! Lower, lower, lower."

They looked surprised and said, "Hey man, you're all right. You can stay for free. Have a good night."

Then, they got into and onto their truck and drove away.

I climbed back into the car and my girlfriend said, "Whew! You sure handled that well."

I told her a brief version of picking up the Native American hitchhiker on the way to Chicago.

The next morning we drove to Taos and checked out the ski resort. It looked too expensive for our budget even though the slopes were still closed so we went back down the mountain. We walked around the tourist section looking at the shops and galleries and then went to a grocery store to stock up on food. In the store a young Indian woman carrying a small baby was looking at the meat selection and when she looked at me I got the impression that she couldn't afford the food and would have liked to take some if she could. About that time Lincoln came running into the store and I dashed out the door carrying an armload of groceries to put him back into the car. The store manager came out to make sure I brought the groceries back into the store, which I did, and I noticed that the young Indian woman had disappeared. My girl friend was really pissed off at me and wouldn't even consider my excuse of creating a diversion for the young girl.

Close to the road that goes up the mountain to the ski resort, we stopped at a small store and I asked about places to camp. The Indian lady there told us about some commercial campsites and told us no there were no hot springs that she knew of in the area but there was a nice place just up a side road with a series of waterfalls falling down high cliffs. We followed the directions and turned left after passing through the gate with the no trespassing sign. We found ourselves in an Eden. The small stream pouring over the cliffs in waterfalls we used for fun showers, and the rock overhangs made excellent shelter from the rain. As I was unpacking the cars a pickup truck drove up to me.

The man inside leaned out and said "So, you are camping here."

I said, "Yes."

And he said, "OK." And backed out and drove away. We stayed for a couple of days of cold, naked, goose bump showers, warm sun and snuggly rainy nights. Unfortunately we disagreed and argued about almost everything else. I no longer remember about what.

The day we left we went back to the tourist area, an old town square. Even though there wasn't a cloud in the sky, I could feel the thunderstorm simmering just beneath the five senses. An old Indian man and his woman were arguing as they passed by, our eyes met with a spark of recognition, and he rejoined his argument with renewed resolve. The thunder still lived. By the time we were driving up the mountain to the west of Taos my budding anger had reached full bloom. My girlfriend was in the car ahead and rather than flinging myself off the mountain in frustration, I pulled into a wide gravel parking area letting her go ahead while I calmed down. As I got out of the car to pace around kicking small rocks and muttering I looked back down into the valley. There over Taos was a huge black thunderstorm spitting lightening from its insides. It had grown or appeared in about one or one-and-a-half hours. This didn't really surprise me but I was awed and amazed by its sheer size and intensity. I got back into the car as I began to calm down. My anger had been completely dwarfed by this magnificent view of awesome fury. A blue and silver pickup truck with a camper top pulled into the pull off and parked about seventy-five feet away.

A sixtyish Indian man leaned out of the passenger window and pointing at me yelled, "Hey, You, Come here!"

As I was the only other person for miles around, I assumed he was talking to me and got back out of the car. Pointing to my chest and arching my eyebrows in a questioning manner, I walked towards the pickup truck. He got out and walked to the rear of the truck. Opening the camper top with a flourish, he revealed the cargo of potato sacks stuffed with fresh peyote that filled the back of the long bed pickup to the top of its camper top.

"How much peyote do you want?" he asked.

Images of my station wagon filled with potato sacks slowly diminish until just one sack remained under a blanket as I was being stopped by the Highway Patrol.

I said, "Wow, that's wonderful, but I'd better just take a couple of buttons. Otherwise, I'm going to get busted."

He opened a sack smiling broadly, refused any money, gave me two nice big buttons, wished me well, and drove off. As he rounded the curve out of sight, I wasn't sure he hadn't just driven out of the mountain itself and had now driven back into it. Anyway, I had peyote.

The road soon leveled out and I took a bite of peyote and a swig of wine and soon caught up to my girlfriend in a very small town with an old adobe mission. We prayed in the mission and had a picnic just across the road. I was ready to press on but she wasn't. We waited for what I don't know until after dark then started to leave town. I started thinking that we might have gotten caught up in a vortex of manifesting thought, so when we passed a car from Tennessee upside down in a ditch and surrounded with onlookers, I just passed it by. My girlfriend stopped and asked me if I thought we should go back, and I said, "No, just keep going and don't look back."

We started climbing another mountain, this time a big one, and my car began to overheat. A leak had developed in the radiator. We stopped at a bar that was about halfway up the mountain to let the car cool off and to ask about motels and campsites. The bartender said there was a motel on the top of the mountain. People were playing pool and as I was leaving the bar someone was about to "break". Suddenly I was filled with foreboding. Instead of God playing with dice, God was playing pool. I felt that each ball represented a person and the ones dropping on the break were the ones who would die. I wanted to run back into the bar to stop the "break" until the feeling dissipated, but I felt that I just might be silly and crazy, so, CRACK, the balls broke from their huddle and as I was walking away I heard some drop into their pockets.

Even though I'd filled my radiator, it was still some miles to the top of the mountain. On the right was another very large thunderstorm. I could feel waves of energy rotating around it like the vanes of a gigantic fan. I noticed that when they passed, the car seemed to have an easier time of the climb so I tried to stay on a vane letting it lift me up the mountain, surfing the shifting energy, so to speak. I also noticed that it was easier on the car's climb when the moths and bugs passed by without hitting it, so I began to "fly" the car through the bugs. This took extreme concentration because I had to see them clairvoyantly or telepathically before I could actually see them, and then I had to move their universe so they would miss the car. Darting all over the road in order to miss them was not an option because it would mess up the vane surfing.

We reached the top of the mountain, and because the thunderstorm had caught up to us, we opted for the motel, where it was OK for Lincoln to stay with us, instead of the nearby campground, where dogs were not allowed. Go figure. At the motel I wrote postcards to about five or six different people. I somehow wrote so all of them together were a message and yet each one was a message in itself. Before we left the motel, I asked the owner if there was any place where I could get my radiator repaired. She said no, but that her husband did heating, air and plumbing and that maybe he could give it a try. He and I soldered the seam shut as best we could and later I got some stop-leak for what little we'd missed.

It was mostly down hill from the mountaintop so there was no worry about overheating. We stopped at a combination general store and post office to get more food, the stop leak, and to mail the postcards. When I mailed the cards the post mistress took them reverently in both hands and thanked me for the honor I had given her by having mailed them from there. I thought that maybe she had started to take some Far Eastern spiritual discipline. A few hours later we reached the small college town near where my girlfriend had been working on a sheep ranch. We spent the night with friends, and the next morning I left to go back east. The road east climbed out of the valley and about three or four miles out of town I saw a truck with its bed missing and the rear corner jacked up so I stopped to help. A medium-sized Indian man was lifting the truck while his wife was putting fist-sized rocks on top of each other until the wheel was held off the ground. At this point, all they needed was to borrow my lug wrench to finish the job. With the new tire in place the man kicked the rickety column of rocks down and off they went. I wondered just how that woman was able to stack about six mostly round rocks with enough accuracy to support that truck. And, of course, how was it that her

husband could be strong enough to lift it? My girlfriend drove up. She had been worried about my mental condition. After seeing that I had it together enough to help some people change a tire, she decided that I would be all right. We said good-by again and as she drove away I looked back into the valley and there was a small thunderstorm raining on the town and bringing tears to my eyes.

I was now released from my connection with the spirit harbored by the thunderstorm and drove back to Tennessee in the regular way enjoying the beautiful scenery with my dog and relaxing as I decompressed along the way. The weather was beautiful. No thunderstorms.

Back in Gatlinburg

I worked in my family's candle shop on the main street of town and sometimes the business was slow so I would just sit and watch the world go slowly by. I thought, at the time, that I should just sit and watch like that on a more regular basis. It used to be all I could do to silently meditate with my eyes closed for a few minutes at church or more frequently when drunk or stoned and relaxed enough that I didn't care if I moved or not. Now that I was back and able to walk more like a person than a zombie and hadn't been living on a steady diet of drugs, I felt good. I could sit without jiggling, and I felt alive again.

After a few days of sitting I decided it was time to see if "the most beautiful woman in town" had broken up with her latest man. They had been together for a couple of years, so they were probably still together, but one never knew around here. I always enjoyed visiting either one of them anyway.

I walked down the street to her store, crossed the street where the Isis charm had leaped from my pocket, looked down the sidewalk where people appeared and disappeared, no one was coming or going that day, so I went into the store. She was looking at the ceiling, or rather through it.

She glanced at me and back at the ceiling and said, "Oh my God. It's all true."

"What's true?" I asked, thinking she was talking about me and my strangeness.

"It's ALL true!" She repeated, waving her hands at the ceiling and walls.

"What's all true?" I asked again, thinking this time that she must be referring to something larger than me.

"EVERYTHING'S ALL TRUE!" She screamed at the ceiling while stretching her arms wide enough to include all of it.

"Aah!" I said as the truth that this was HER epiphany finally dawned on me.

I just walked back across the street. She was busy.